"You're not looking for your son. You're looking for a fresh start," Rebecca said.

Cole released her and stepped back as if honesty had hit a nerve. "Don't pretend to know me." He loomed over her. "I traveled over a thousand miles to find my son."

His hot breath warmed her cheek. His face was so close, the heat of his body beckoned her.

For her—his—son's sake, she wished she could believe Cole, but she knew if she allowed him to work his way into their lives, then left, it could be devastating. "A thousand miles is nothing compared to a lifetime of responsibility."

"I'm not leaving." Cole cupped her face in his rough hands and stared into her eyes. The contact was jolting. Time slowed to a maddening crawl and the world drifted away. There were only the two of them.

She should hate him, but she didn't. All she felt was worry, guilt…and longing. The icy loneliness that had encased her heart for so long began to melt. And then suddenly she knew. She wasn't just protecting her son's heart, but her own as well.

Praise for Mary Burton's first book
A BRIDE FOR McCAIN

"This is a delightful Western romp...
A great first book for this new author!"
—*Old Book Barn Gazette*

"Warm-hearted, charming, and sweet,
this is a delightful tale."
—*Romantic Times Magazine*

"It will leave you yearning for more
from this talented author."
—*Rendezvous*

"Newcomer Mary Burton is a delightful surprise
for Western romance fans as her genial tale...
will fully beguile readers."
—*Affaire de Coeur*

The Colorado Bride
Harlequin Historical #570—July 2001

MARY BURTON

THE COLORADO BRIDE

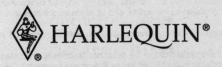

HARLEQUIN®

TORONTO • NEW YORK • LONDON
AMSTERDAM • PARIS • SYDNEY • HAMBURG
STOCKHOLM • ATHENS • TOKYO • MILAN • MADRID
PRAGUE • WARSAW • BUDAPEST • AUCKLAND

ISBN 0-373-29170-1

THE COLORADO BRIDE

Please address questions and book requests to:
Harlequin Reader Service
U.S.: 3010 Walden Ave., P.O. Box 1325, Buffalo, NY 14269
Canadian: P.O. Box 609, Fort Erie, Ont. L2A 5X3

For Alex and Julia

Chapter One

1882

Strangers stuck out in White Stone, Colorado like snow in July.

Cole McGuire reined in his horse at the outskirts of the dusty, near dried-up town. He was conscious that farmers had stopped unloading their goods from their wagons; women were staring and yanking their children close to their skirts; and the handful of cattlemen had moved to the edge of the sun-bleached boardwalk to get a better look at him.

Cole tugged his wide-brimmed hat down, shielding his eyes against the biting sun and the blatant curiosity. Foolish to think he could have slipped into town unnoticed.

His body was long and lean, honed by years of soldiering. His gray duster hung open, revealing a black shirt, army issue pants and worn leather chaps that brushed the tops of scuffed boots. Thick stubble blanketed his square jaw and his black hair draped over his coat collar. A well-oiled rifle lay across his saddle.

Cole assessed the odd collection of weathered buildings, which were as colorless as the people. The Methodist church had never gotten its steeple; Gene Applegate's mercantile displayed the same hair tonic advertisement it had three years ago; and a half-dozen businesses that had once prospered were now boarded up.

What the hell had happened?

Three years ago, Robert Sinclair's Lucky Star Mine had been giving up five thousand dollars worth of gold a day and White Stone had been teaming with people and new construction. The town's population had swelled past ten thousand and there had been talk that Sinclair planned to build a fancy courthouse with big white columns.

But none of that had happened. Fact was, the town looked like it was barely hanging on.

The town's fading prosperity didn't soothe Cole's unease. He looked over his shoulder toward the parched grasslands and longed to ride back across them away from old memories and a town that had never wanted him.

Instead, he coaxed his horse forward. This homecoming wasn't about him.

As he rode down Main Street, a portly woman wearing a black dress and a hat sporting a peacock feather stared boldly at him. Her thick lips curled into a frown. He remembered her—Gladys Applegate. Her husband owned the mercantile and she was the town's self-appointed guardian of right and wrong.

Cole touched the brim of his hat, keeping his head low and his gaze averted as he coaxed his horse on. He wasn't up to answering any nosy questions.

He dismounted in front of the Rosebud Saloon and tied the reins to the post. As he strode toward the boardwalk, his spurs jangled softly mingling with piano music that drifted through the saloon's swinging doors. The Rosebud had a freshly whitewashed exterior and a new sign complete with gilded letters and a painted red rose. The corner of Cole's mouth kicked up. No matter how bad the times, Seth Osborne, the saloon owner, always managed to turn a profit.

A burly man strode out of the saloon's red swinging doors, and bumped into Cole. Clad in denims and a white shirt, Stan Farthing was fatter than Cole remembered, but he still wore a droopy mustache and likely still owned the livery.

"Pardon," Stan said before he glanced at Cole. Recognition then anger flashed in his weary eyes.

Ten years ago, Stan had wrongly accused Cole of stealing. The two had fought and Cole had beaten the devil out of him. "Stan."

"I'd hoped we'd never see you again," he snarled.

Cole's hand slid to his pistol. He'd ridden hard these last few days and his patience was paper thin. "I don't appreciate your tone."

Stan assessed Cole's six-foot, two-inch frame, then as if realizing he'd bitten off more than he could chew, softened his scowl. "Do us all a favor and don't stay in White Stone long."

Stan hurried down the street past several more people who had listened to the exchange. Cole glared back at them, waiting until their gazes dropped before he reached for the swinging doors.

A barefoot boy, no more than ten, with ragged clothes and a dirty face sauntered up to him. "I'll water your horse for a penny, mister." The boy had hollowed features and blue eyes wise beyond their years.

Cole paused. He had never paid much attention to children—until recently. Now, he noticed them in every town he passed through. He wondered when this kid had eaten last.

Cole reached in his pocket, dug out a nickel and

pressed it into the boy's grimy palm. "Just guard him for me."

The boy inspected the coin then tucked it in his pants pocket. "Hey, you need anything else, come to me. I know how to find anything in this town. Just ask for Dusty."

Cole nodded. "I'm not planning on staying that long."

Dusty positioned himself in front of Cole's black horse. "Just the same, I'm here if you need me."

"Thanks, kid."

Cole pushed open the saloon doors. The smell of stale whiskey welcomed him, as did cigar smoke, so thick it choked out the afternoon sun.

The odors triggered memories of years spent watching his ma sling drinks and saunter off into the back room with any cowboy who had two bits. He had hated the Rosebud from the instant he'd first laid eyes on it.

He was eighteen when his ma had passed on and he'd packed up what little he had and joined the army. There he'd found a code of honor and learned he had a nose for tracking and a talent for leading men. Three months ago, he'd retired with distinction, the rank of captain.

Yet, as he stood in this room, he felt fourteen again. Forgotten, alone and angry.

Cole chose a table in a dark corner and tossed

his hat on the sticky wooden surface. He sat straight in the chair, his back to the wall and slid damp palms over muscular thighs. He itched to be done with his business.

A red-haired barmaid with tired eyes sauntered over, and set a bottle of whiskey and a tumbler down in front of him. "You look thirsty."

Cole poured his whiskey with deliberate slowness. "Is Seth here?"

The beauty mark painted on the corner of her mouth twitched. "Who's asking?"

Cole pulled out a half dollar from his vest pocket and put it on the table. He edged it toward her, keeping his fingers over the tarnished coin. "Tell him Cole's back."

Her finger skimmed over the top of her low-cut bodice. "Anything you say, sugar."

Cole flipped the coin in the air and the barmaid snatched it with practiced ease. She tucked the coin in her ample cleavage and strolled toward Seth's office.

He stared into the whiskey's amber depths, not quite able to stomach the brew or the memories. He couldn't get out of this town fast enough.

"I'd have bet fifty dollars that I'd never see your sorry face around here again," a familiar voice cackled.

Seth Osborne limped toward his table. Ever

since Cole could remember, Seth had been old. His wrinkled features, long gray hair and hunched shoulders had been a fixture in the saloon since White Stone was little more than a mud hole.

Cole rose and extended his hand. Age and experience had taught him that even though the old man had been hard on him at times, he had always been fair to him. "Seth."

Seth squinted as he studied Cole closer. "You look harder every time I see you."

"Likewise."

"Staying long?"

"Long enough to talk to Lily."

Shock then sadness doused the sparkle in Seth's eyes. "You never heard."

"Heard what?"

"Cole, she died over two years ago."

Seth's words slammed into Cole's stomach like a fist. Automatically, his hand slid into his pocket holding the rumpled, beautifully scripted letter Lily had paid another woman to write. He'd read its words a thousand times, memorizing every detail. It had been dated December 12, 1879, but he'd only received it two months ago. In it, Lily had told him she'd conceived their child during his last stay in town.

Her news had rocked him. At first he'd refused to believe it. But as the shock had worn off, he couldn't deny the possibility that the child was his. Determined that his child would not grow up in the back room of a saloon as he had, he'd delayed his dreams of mining in California and come to White Stone.

His fingers tightened into fists. "When did she die?"

"January of '80."

Cole eased down into his seat.

"I know you two was close," Seth offered.

"Yea." They'd been friends and lovers since she'd come to work in the Rosebud fifteen years ago. He reached for the glass of whiskey.

"She talked about you from time to time."

Cole drained the tumbler, focusing on the way it burned his throat. "How'd she die?"

Seth's glance slipped away. "It don't really matter, does it? It's been over two years."

His fingers tightened around the glass. "It matters."

The old-timer sighed. "She died in childbirth."

Seth mumbled a few words of sympathy, but they didn't register in Cole's mind. All he could think about was that Lily was gone. Unable to concentrate, he refilled the glass and gulped it down.

Seth's eyes clouded with worry. "Careful. That stuff you're drinking is strong enough to knock a mule on its ass."

Cole stared at the peeling label on the bottle. "Lily said I was the father of her baby."

Seth straightened. "Lily was known to whore, son."

Cole hadn't loved Lily, but he'd laughed with her, kissed her, been intimate with her and he wasn't going to let their child be forgotten. "If she said the baby was mine, it was. Where's the child?"

"Ain't no telling who the father was."

Cole persisted. "Her letter was signed 'Mrs. Curtis Taylor for Lily Davis.'"

Seth frowned. "Leave Lily buried in the past where she belongs."

Cole flexed his fingers. "Where can I find Mrs. Curtis Taylor? Maybe she's got answers for me."

Seth cleared his throat. "It won't do you any good talking to Mrs. Taylor. Do yourself a favor and move on."

He pushed his chair back from the table and stood. "I'll find her myself if you won't tell me."

Seth blocked his path. He knew Cole well enough to know he wasn't bluffing. "She'll be by any minute. She delivers pies every day."

Right then, the saloon patrons hooted and hollered, distracting Cole from his thoughts.

Seth looked toward the swinging doors. The

hard lines etched in the corners of his eyes softened. "That'll be her now."

Cole shifted for a better view of Mrs. Curtis Taylor. He muttered an oath when he saw her. Damn, it was Sinclair's daughter Rebecca.

She was just as petite as he remembered. Delicate. The princess in the ivory tower. When he'd come to town three years ago, she'd just married and was in Denver on her honeymoon.

Calico, not silk, now hugged her slender waist and accentuated the curve of her breasts. She no longer wore her hair in ringlets but had pinned her blond strands back into a neat topknot. Wisps of hair fell loose and framed her rounded face, full lips and high cheekbones. Her light-blue eyes no longer sparkled with the giddy laughter of a young girl, but reflected the confidence of a woman.

Lovely, he thought, then dismissed the idea. Men like him only dreamed about women like her. Besides, he didn't dally with married women.

Cole took a second glance at her simple attire. Sinclair had spoiled his only child. She had lived in a world of fine parties and fancy boarding schools and spent more money on a single dress than he'd earned in a year. So, why was she delivering pies to a saloon?

Ignoring the hoots and hollers, Rebecca walked up to Seth. The scent of roses and cinnamon caressed Cole's senses and he felt the familiar tightening each time he'd seen her in town.

"Good morning, Seth," she said, her voice clear and bright.

He might never have stopped staring at her if he hadn't seen the rustle of her skirts and caught sight of the young toddler clinging to her side. The boy's blond hair curled at the ends like Rebecca's had when she was younger, but his skin was darker and his eyes a rich brown. Her son, he assumed.

Seth's smile broadened. "Right on time as usual."

"You're my best customer. I'd never let you down." Laughter rang in her clear voice.

Seth winked at the boy. "Hi, Mac."

The boy grinned and popped his thumb in his mouth as he edged closer to his mother.

Rebecca's gaze shifted to Cole. She studied him in a measuring way as if she were trying to place him, but could not. Cole wasn't surprised she didn't remember him. He'd swept out saloons and worked in her father's mine.

Rebecca laid her hand protectively on her son's shoulder, then glanced down at the wicker basket in her hands. "Three apple pies and two cherry, just like you asked."

"Thanks," Seth said straightening.

She kept her eyes on Seth, carefully avoiding

Cole's gaze. "I'll put the pies on the bar and leave. I promised Mac a piece of candy from the mercantile." She and Mac headed toward the long, mahogany bar.

"Thanks, Rebecca. See you same time tomorrow."

Cole wondered why the old man hadn't introduced them. Rebecca had already unpacked three pies when he spoke up. "Mrs. Taylor, I want to talk to you."

She raised another pie out of the basket. "Do I know you, mister?"

"The name's Cole McGuire."

She dropped the cherry pie on the floor. The tin pan clanked against the floor splattering bits of cherry everywhere. "Cole McGuire," she whispered.

She stared into his eyes as if seeing him for the first time. Her gaze dropped to his jaw covered in a week's worth of growth to his sweat-stained bandana past his worn chaps and finally to his mud-splattered boots. He'd not bathed in over a week and suspected a good inch of trail dust coated his body. Her pert nose wrinkled and she pulled the boy behind her skirts, now stained with the ruined cherry pie.

He reckoned she compared him to the miners who had worked in her father's mines, no better than the pack mules that hauled wagons. He kept all traces of emotion from his face even though an old, raw anger roiled inside him. For one split second he was again the town whore's son and she the unattainable rich man's daughter. He swallowed his anger. "You remember me?"

"Yes."

Seth cleared his throat. "Here let me clean that mess up, Rebecca." He turned to Cole. "There ain't much she can tell you."

Cole ignored Seth, his sights on Rebecca. "You wrote a letter for Lily Davis a couple of years ago."

With trembling hands, Rebecca pulled the last pie tin out of her basket and put it on the bar. "I thought you'd ignored the letter."

"It only found me two months ago."

She moistened her lips. "I never thought you'd come."

Seth handed Rebecca her empty basket. "I told Cole that Lily died right after the birthing and that I don't remember much else."

She glanced at Seth then back at Cole. "I don't know what I could add." He detected a note of steel in her voice.

"I want to know what happened to Lily's baby."

She clutched the handle of the basket, her

knuckles turning white. "I only wrote the one letter for her."

Her evasive answer pricked him like a thorn. He closed the distance between them in three strides. "You must know something," he insisted. "Lily was a proud woman and she wouldn't have asked just anybody to write a letter for her."

The old man coughed. "It was a long time ago."

"Was the child a boy or girl?" Cole persisted.

Rebecca paled. "A boy."

A son. Lily had carried his son. Cole cleared his throat. His heart thundered with wild excitement and for an instant he savored a moment of pure happiness. "Where is he? Is he alive?"

She stepped back taking her son's hand. "I'm sorry, but I can't help you and I really must be going."

He grabbed her by the arm, forcing her to stay. The little boy whimpered at Cole's sudden movement and clung to his mother's skirts, sensing danger. "I want to know *more,* Mrs. Taylor. I must know more."

She tried to tug her arm free—his touch seemingly offending her—but he wouldn't release her. "The baby's gone, Mr. McGuire."

Silence hung between them. "My son died?"

"Yes," she said her voice suddenly soft, full of emotion.

His shoulders slumped and he released her. He'd told himself he was returning to White Stone out of duty and honor. Now he realized he'd wanted this child and a family of his own. His entire life had been spent either in the back room of a saloon or in army barracks. He'd grown tired of his gypsy life. This child had been his chance at a new beginning.

He tried to picture the child over a thousand miles of dusty trails. And now he was gone. His insides ached. He wanted to ride as far away from White Stone as he could.

"I'm so very sorry," she whispered.

Cole stared into her watery blue eyes, unable to speak.

"Mama," Mac said. "Candy."

"In a minute, honey."

Something about the boy grabbed his attention. He looked into the brown eyes and, for an instant, pictured his son who would have been about that age if he'd lived.

Rebecca shielded the boy with her skirt. "I really do have to get going."

Seth quickly escorted her to the door. "I'll talk to you later."

She stared at the old man a long moment, then squeezed his hand. "Thanks, Seth."

Cole's instincts had saved him more than once

on the prairies when he'd been hunting renegades. He never ignored them. And right now instinct told him something was wrong.

Cole strode to the saloon window and watched Rebecca, her son nestled on her hip as she hurried past Dusty, past the mercantile and down the boardwalk. Wherever she was going, she was in a mighty big rush.

Seth came up behind him. "Maybe it's best to leave well enough alone, Cole. Mrs. Taylor doesn't need any more worries."

Cole had an unexplainable urge to know more. "What happened to Sinclair's money?"

"Rebecca's husband stole the profits from the mines and ran off. She was forced to close the Lucky Star when there wasn't money to shore up the mining shafts."

"That explains why the town is drying up." He rubbed the thick, black stubble on his chin. "Where's her husband now?"

"Shot dead in a Denver gaming hall a couple of years back."

Cole couldn't summon any sadness at the news. "That must have been rough on her."

Seth grunted. "She's better off. Curtis Taylor was a gambler and a con artist whose thieving nearly destroyed this town and Rebecca. He left her with only pennies to her name."

"Looks like she's managing."

The old man's eyes shone with pride. "She's no delicate flower like everybody first thought. She's proven herself to be a good woman and a fine mother."

"Surprised another man hasn't snapped her up."

"Every man in town's tried to court her in the last two years with no luck. She keeps 'em all at arm's length and is content to raise her son alone and run her boarding house."

The back of Cole's scalp itched just like it did before an ambush. He picked up his hat from the table and traced the black brim with his finger. He strode toward the swinging doors and pushed them open.

Seth came up behind him. "Cole, the best thing you can do for yourself is ride out of White Stone. There ain't nothing for you here."

And go where? California had lost its appeal. "It's as good a place as any to live."

"White Stone's dying. A young man like you needs a town that's got more to offer." A hint of desperation laced his words.

"I was thinking about staying for a while."

Seth coughed. "You was?"

"Why not?"

Seth glanced in Rebecca's direction. "Well, uh,

you're welcome to your old room,'' he said nudging him back inside the Rosebud.

Cole shook his head. "Thanks. But I reckon I'll stay at Mrs. Taylor's boarding house.''

Chapter Two

*C*ole McGuire *had returned.*

Unshed tears burned Rebecca's throat as she hugged Mac close and hurried down the boardwalk toward home. For two years, she'd thought herself safe and that he'd never return to White Stone to claim his son. Now, he was here.

She cursed the day she'd written that letter to him.

Rebecca remembered writing it as if it were yesterday....

Curtis had run off only days before and she hadn't been able to muster the strength to face anyone.

So she didn't respond to Lily's persistent knocking on her front door, expecting her to give up and leave her alone just like everyone else had.

"Anybody home?" Lily shouted as she opened the front door. Her husky voice echoed down dusty

hallways. True to form, the saloon singer sounded as brazen as Delilah herself. "Mrs. Taylor?"

Rebecca sat at the small kitchen table, a half-cup of cold coffee in front of her. Her eyes ached from crying. She glanced up at the tall woman who wore a lemon silk dress with layers of lace around the collar and cuffs. She had hair as black as ink, brown eyes and like Rebecca, she was pregnant, her time only two months away.

An angry dismissal sprang to mind, but years of etiquette kept Rebecca's tongue in check. She pushed herself to her feet, her hand cupping her swollen belly. "May I ask what brings you here?"

"You look like you haven't slept in days."

"Did you come here to critique my appearance?"

"No. I need your services."

Lily snapped open the curtains and let sunshine pour over unwashed dishes in the sink. "I need you to write me a letter."

Rebecca squinted against the glaring light. "This isn't a good time. Maybe you could come back tomorrow."

"I wouldn't impose normally, but I need a letter written to my baby's daddy. I'm willing to pay." Lily set two bits on the table.

Fresh tears burned Rebecca's puffy eyes. A

whore was paying her for her services. How could she have fallen so far so fast? "Please just leave."

"Word is you could use the money."

Sympathy echoed in Lily's voice. Unable to bear her pity Rebecca faced Lily. "I don't need anything from you or anybody else in this town."

The corners of Lily's mouth kicked up. "Well at least you're getting mad. That's a step in the right direction." Her eyes softened. "I know this is a hard time for you." Lily laid her hands on Rebecca's shoulders and guided her into the library toward an overstuffed chair. "But you got to learn to take care of yourself."

Rebecca sank into the chair. Her marriage, her world, everything she'd believed in was crumbling. "I don't know how to take care of myself much less a baby."

Lily marched to the window and opened the curtains, letting light flood over shelves of dusty leather-bound books that had belonged to Robert Sinclair. "Honey, you got this big old house just sitting empty. If I was you, I'd turn it into an inn. Lord knows White Stone needs a decent place for folks to stay and with the stage coach coming through a few times a month, you're guaranteed customers."

"Maybe."

"You gotta stop feeling sorry for yourself. You got a baby on the way to think about."

Fresh tears filled her reddened eyes. "How do I pick up the pieces and go on?"

"You ain't got any choice."

Rebecca wanted to escape to her bedroom and pull the covers over her head, but she knew Lily was right. She smoothed her hand over her rounded belly. A warm feeling tugged at her heart and the mournful haze that had clouded her mind began to clear. If she didn't fight for herself and her baby, no one else would. "I do have five extra rooms."

"Now you're talking. And I'm willing to be your first customer."

For the first time in a string of days, life didn't seem hopeless. Rebecca went to her father's old desk and sat down. She reached for a creamy white piece of paper embossed with Mrs. Curtis Taylor and dipped the nub of her pen in the ink. She met Lily's direct gaze. "You said you needed a letter written." She cleared her throat. "For two bits."

Lily laid her money on the desk. Her eyes sparkled with approval. "I think you're gonna do just fine."

And Rebecca knew then, somehow she would.

Lily dictated her thoughts to her baby's father,

and Rebecca wrote every word down. And from then on the whore and the rich girl became friends.

Over the next few weeks bitter January winds blew as the two women spent hours together, sharing their fears and hopes.

And then Rebecca went into labor. Lily held her hand, offering words of comfort during the long agonizing labor. Rebecca's baby—a girl—was stillborn. Lily stayed at her side during the next few agonizing days, offering solace to Rebecca for her lost child.

Then Lily's time came and Rebecca, still grief-stricken and exhausted, dragged herself out of bed to be at her friend's side. The birthing had been quick and easy, but then Lily had started to hemorrhage and within hours she was gone.

Engorged with milk and her heart aching, Rebecca held her friend's limp hand, stunned at how fragile life was. She could barely believe Lily and her own baby were gone. She didn't know how long she sat in the darkened room alone before the cries of Lily's child penetrated the darkness around her.

She stared at Lily's infant son still covered with afterbirth as it kicked and squirmed on the bed next to his dead mother. She picked up the boy and held him close. She whispered soothing words and rocked him back and forth.

It seemed only right that Rebecca care for Lily's child until Cole came for him.

But when she took the baby to her breast and suckled him, her heart filled with unimaginable happiness. In that instant, the boy had become her son and she knew she'd never give him up.

"I'm sorry, Lily. Mac is mine now!"

"Miz Rebecca!"

Startled from her thoughts, Rebecca looked up to find Sheriff Ernie Wade standing in her path. She'd almost walked right into the grizzly bear of a man who smiled down at her. His shoulder-length hair and close-cropped beard resembled the color of well-traveled snow. The man wore faded denims, a plaid shirt and a dented tin star on his chest.

Rebecca hugged Mac tighter to her breast, impatient to get him home. "Afternoon, Sheriff."

"Miz Rebecca, you're looking mighty fine today."

"Thanks." She started to leave.

"I was just thinking about the Fourth of July picnic. You know it's next week?"

"Yes." She didn't want to sound rude as she tried to step around him, but she had to hurry. "Perhaps, we could talk later."

"Well, we could, but what I got to say won't take but a minute."

She wanted to scream. She needed to get home. "What is it, Sheriff?"

"I was thinking you and Mac could come with me to the festivities."

She tried to step around him. "Sure, that would be fine."

His eyes brightened. "You mean it?"

"Absolutely. Perhaps we can talk about it later. I really need to get home."

"Oh, sure. You get home and I'll stop by later and talk over our plans."

"Great."

She nestled Mac on her hip and quickened her pace across the dusty street, her mind brimming with worries. Instinct told her to take her son and run as far away from White Stone as she could. If she sold what remained of her mother's silver, she could reach Denver or Cheyenne and stay hidden for months.

Rebecca opened the gate to the picket fence surrounding the wood frame house built by her father. Just looking at its whitewashed exterior, gabled roof and wraparound porch soothed her nerves. Her most treasured and difficult memories were as much a part of the house as the timber and nails.

Rebecca yanked open the front door and the

smell of freshly baked cookies drifted out to greet her. Bess. When Mac was a baby, she had hired the widowed Bess Gunston, a no-nonsense pioneer from Kentucky who at seventeen had followed her husband to White Stone twenty years ago when he'd come in search of gold. The prospector had never struck it rich and when he died, Bess had needed a place to live. Rebecca had needed the help and what had started off as an arrangement grew into a deep friendship.

"That you, Rebecca?" Bess called.

"Yes. I'm home."

"Bess! Bess!" Mac squealed.

Rebecca set her son down and watched him run toward the kitchen. He moved like a big boy now, no longer a baby.

When she reached the kitchen, she found Mac hugging Bess's skirts. The older woman stood at the kitchen table, her meaty hands buried in a mound of bread dough. Flour smudged her blue homespun dress. "I just put a pie outside to cool and a loaf of bread like you asked. You know that urchin boy is gonna steal 'em."

Rebecca smoothed a curl off her face with a trembling hand. "His name is Dusty. And he won't take charity."

"So you put out food for him to steal."

"He's got to eat."

"Cookie!" Mac squealed.

The little boy's brown eyes, olive complexion and blond hair reminded her so much of Lily—the friend she'd just betrayed with her lies. Guilt tugged at Rebecca's heart.

Pushing the unwelcome blame aside, Rebecca went to a blue jar and fished out a large sugar cookie. Mac heard the rattle of the jar and hurried to Rebecca. He clapped his hands and laughed. She knelt and handed him the cookie, content to watch him gobble the treat. She brushed crumbs from his rosy cheeks then stroked his silken hair. Maternal pride welled inside her. "How's that cookie, big boy?"

He cupped her face with his small, sticky hands and grinned, revealing his six teeth. "Good."

Bess shoved the heel of her hands into its spongy dough. "It ain't smart to hand out sweets so close to lunch."

"Bess, Mac and I are leaving town."

Her words met stunned silence. "What are you talking about?"

"He's back."

"Who's back?"

"Cole McGuire."

Bess hissed in a sharp breath. "You sure it's him?"

"I spoke to him at the saloon not ten minutes ago."

"What's he doing in White Stone?"

"Looking for Lily."

Worry lines creased Bess's brow. "Oh, lands. He got the letter."

"Yes." Rebecca's thoughts turned to finding her luggage—the set she'd bought on her honeymoon. Where was it?

"Cole came looking for his child?"

"Yes." *Luggage, downstairs closet, top shelf.*

"Does he know about Mac?"

Distracted, Rebecca strode toward the hallway closet without answering. Standing on tiptoe, she pulled a dusty brown satchel down. She thought about Cole's dark, dangerous gaze burning into her and she pushed back a feeling of panic.

"Does he know about Mac?" Bess had followed her out of the kitchen and spoke behind her.

"I told him the baby died."

"Rebecca!"

She jerked a large square bag down to the floor. "I know it was wrong, but I was so afraid."

"Honey, it's a matter of time before he finds out. Too many people in town know."

"That's why Mac and I are leaving."

"But White Stone is your home."

"My home is with *my* child."

Rebecca hurried to the kitchen to check on Mac who now sat on the floor. He'd smashed his cookie into small bits and was now eating the crumbs one by one.

"What if he follows you?" Bess demanded.

"I'll make sure he doesn't find us," she said turning back to face her.

Bess sighed. "Honey, you're heading down a dangerous path."

Rebecca shook her head, more worried than before. "I have to protect Mac."

"Cole is the boy's father," Bess warned.

"That doesn't mean he's fit to raise Mac. Look at Dusty's pa. He deserted that boy two months ago."

"But Cole ain't been given a chance with his son."

"Whose side are you on?" Rebecca asked.

"I'm on your side. But you best think long and hard before you start lying to Cole McGuire."

"If I tell him the truth, he will take Mac from me." Rebecca smacked her fist against her thigh. Life had finally become good, happy and safe again. And now this.

"Think about Lily," Bess asked softly. "She would have wanted Cole to know his son."

Bess was right, but Rebecca couldn't admit it.

"It's not a simple matter anymore. Too much time has passed."

"Can you live with yourself after it's all said and done?"

For an instant, Rebecca wavered. "I'll have to."

Bess remained silent.

Her friend's silence magnified her guilt. "Men like Cole or Curtis aren't the father type. They grow tired of responsibility and leave."

"Rebecca, I don't like this."

She pressed her hands to her flushed cheeks. "Please, don't argue. I need your help."

Bess' worry lines softened. "You know I'll stand by you."

Rebecca nodded. "Then help me pack."

"All right."

The bell on the front door rang. Rebecca started. Fearing it was Cole, she peered down the hallway through the screened front door. She saw four women from the sewing circle. In front of the group, stood a short, portly woman dressed in black and wearing a hat sporting a jaunty feather.

Rebecca groaned. "Mrs. Applegate and her army. What do they want?"

"Hello? Is anyone home?" Mrs. Applegate called out.

Bess snorted. "Likely she's heard about Cole."

"I suppose I better find out. Take Mac up the

back stairs and start pulling out clothes. As soon as I get rid of her, I'll join you.''

''Sure thing, dear,'' Bess said.

Mrs. Applegate called out louder, ''Is anyone home?''

Rebecca hurried down the hallway. Gladys Applegate was the unofficial leader of the town women and ran the ladies' church circle with an iron hand. No one disputed her word.

Behind her was Prudence Weatherby, a reed thin widow with piercing close-set eyes who was the town schoolteacher. Next to her stood Madeline Richards and Olivia Farthing. Sisters, they were both short and stocky with rosy cheeks and red hair.

Rebecca managed a smile. ''What can I do for you today?''

Mrs. Applegate swept into the foyer, her eyes sparkling with an uncommon twinkle reserved for those times when she had an unusually good piece of gossip to share. ''Have you heard the news? Cole McGuire is back.''

''Yes. I ran into him at the saloon.''

Mrs. Applegate looked vaguely disappointed. Gossip spread fast in White Stone and Mrs. Applegate enjoyed delivering it. ''I was hoping to spare you any unnecessary shock.''

''Thank you.''

Olivia cleared her throat. "My Stan told me Cole's at the Rosebud Saloon right now, likely drinking whiskey like there's no tomorrow."

Prudence wrinkled her nose. "You'd have thought ten years in the army and a handful of medals would have straightened that man out, but I guess not."

Madeline pursed her lips. "Once a bad seed, always a bad seed. But then, what can you expect with a ma like his?"

Fresh fears churned inside Rebecca. "Mrs. Applegate, ladies, can we talk later? I've got to—"

"Does Cole know about Mac?" Mrs. Applegate said.

"No, not yet."

The women sighed collectively and nodded. Mrs. Applegate leaned closer. "Good. We've come to help."

Rebecca frowned. "There's nothing you can do. Mac and I are leaving town."

The ladies stepped into the foyer. They stood side by side, like Amazons ready to do battle.

Prudence thrust out her bony chin. "You can't leave White Stone. This is your home."

"I have no choice," Rebecca said.

"Of course you do," said Mrs. Applegate. "Is it true you told him the baby died?"

Bunched muscles in her back tightened another

notch. "Yes. But it's just a matter of time before he finds out I lied."

Mrs. Applegate cocked an eyebrow. "Not if we tell everyone to keep quiet. One word from us and your secret is safe forever."

Rebecca pressed her palms to her flushed cheeks. "Do you think they would?"

"It won't be hard to convince everyone to keep silent. Cole made too many enemies when he lived here."

Rebecca drew in a deep breath. "Should I help?"

"No. He'll surely guess something is wrong if he sees you running around talking to folks. I'll go over to the dry goods store and have a talk with my husband. He'll pass the word to anyone I miss. Prudence can reach the rest of the sewing circle and Madeline and Olivia can start talking to the folks on the street."

Sickened, Rebecca wished there was another way. "Do you really think it'll work?"

"Absolutely." Mrs. Applegate clapped her hands together. "Ladies, we must be off. We've got a lot to do in a short period of time."

A hum of whispers buzzed around the women as they hurried down the front steps.

Rebecca lingered at the doorway, her head resting against the doorjamb. The encounter with Mrs.

Applegate and the other ladies left her feeling drained, lifeless. As much as she hated the lies, she feared the truth more and what it could do to her family.

She walked down the hallway to where the musty leather pieces of luggage sat. The day she'd bought them in Denver, she'd been so filled with hope and happiness. She thought then that nothing could stand in her way.

Now she knew differently. Her life barely resembled the dreams she'd once had. She touched a small tassel hanging from the satchel's smooth handle. She tightened her fist around it.

Surrender was not an option. Mac depended on her and she didn't have the luxury of sequestering herself in this house and locking out the world. She had to fight, use whatever weapon she could to keep him safe, and if that meant lying to Cole, then so be it.

A loud knock on the front door startled her out of her thoughts. She turned, expecting to see Mrs. Applegate and the other ladies.

It was Cole McGuire.

Chapter Three

Rebecca caught her breath.

Cole McGuire stood on the porch, just on the other side of the screened door. His muscular frame dominated the space around him, his gray range coat tucked carelessly behind his holster. She felt as if the ground shifted under her.

For an instant, her worst fears were realized.

Dear Lord, he'd found out the truth.

Cole, no longer a lanky boy, was a man now, with muscular legs and shoulders, a desperado, ready to fight, even kill for what he wanted.

He'd been daunting back in the saloon; now he looked truly menacing.

She swallowed, her throat as dry as dust.

Rebecca considered barring the door and running. But as tempted as she was, she knew he'd catch her. There was no place to go; no place to hide.

She clenched trembling hands at her sides and rose to her feet. As she walked toward the door, she prayed Bess would keep Mac upstairs until she could get rid of Cole. The less he saw of the boy the better.

She didn't open the screened door, unwilling to let him in her house. "I didn't expect to see you again, Mr. McGuire. I thought you were leaving town."

He smiled slowly, as if he were the cat and she the mouse. "I changed my mind."

She moistened her dried lips. "What made you change it?"

He grinned. "You."

Light-headed, she struggled to keep her voice steady. "Me? Whatever did I do?"

"I reckon it was your kind words back at the saloon. I can't say I've had many good words tossed my way in White Stone."

She imagined a patronizing glint in his green eyes. "It was nothing."

"Losing a son, even one a fellow never met can cut a man to his soul. I doubt I'll ever forget the look on your face when you spoke to me. You understood."

Cole's words pierced her heart.

"I was just being neighborly," she said softly.

His eyes were devoid of compassion. They were the eyes of a hunter.

God made men like Cole for a reason. They were the warriors. But she knew men like him weren't meant to be fathers. She wondered if he was even capable of love.

He stepped back and surveyed the front porch and rockers. "This sure is a fine place you got here."

"Thank you."

He flicked the Vacant sign with his gloved finger making it swing. "I was thinking about staying a week or two."

"In White Stone?" she croaked.

"Yea. And I'm gonna need a room."

She almost choked on the words. "A room?"

"You do have one don't you?"

The Vacant sign creaked back and forth puncturing the silence. "Yes, of course."

"Then I'll take one. How much?"

Her heart thundered in her chest. *Go away!*

She cleared her throat. "The rate's three dollars a night. Breakfast and dinner are extra. And I expect the first night to be paid up front." She'd just tripled her daily rate to discourage him.

"Kind of high."

"Everything's expensive in Colorado."

He stared at her. "So, it seems."

Squirming under his gaze, she reached for the front door handle. "Seth's got rooms at the saloon.

They're more reasonable. I'm sure you'd be more comfortable there anyway.''

"You don't seem too anxious for my business. Something wrong?"

Her throat tightened. ''It's not that. I just thought you didn't like this place.''

He stepped closer; only the unlocked door separated them. "You never imagined you'd have a saloon brat sleeping under your roof, did you Rebecca *Sinclair* Taylor?"

His bitterness surprised her. A denial sprang to her lips, but she caught herself before she spoke it. She deserved his wrath, if not for snobbery then for deceit.

Mac's laughter echoed through the house. He sounded close. Afraid he'd come thundering down the stairs, she opened the door and stepped outside to put a barrier between the boy and Cole. "Don't be silly.''

He smiled, or rather snarled. "Since I arrived in White Stone, I've felt real unwelcome."

Rebecca dug her fingernails into her palms. ''There was a time when you stirred up a lot of trouble.''

"A lifetime ago."

"Folks have a long memory in White Stone."

He pinned her with his gaze, again the hunter closing in on his prey. "So it seems."

Inches separated them. The smell of whiskey and an earthy masculine scent filled her senses.

She didn't dare ask what thoughts lurked behind his dark eyes. Guilt welled inside her. "I'm sorry I didn't have better news for you about your son."

He stepped back. "Me, too."

Grateful for the distance between them, she stepped away from the door. "I've got work to do. If you'll excuse me?"

He looked past her and saw the luggage. "Going somewhere?"

"A little spring cleaning."

"It's nearly July."

"I'm late."

His gaze shifted back to her. Seconds passed like years. Then he pushed past her into the house, his shoulder brushing against hers. Every muscle in her body constricted.

He acted as if he owned the place. He pulled off his hat. "The house was half built when Ma and I moved to White Stone. I used to sit for hours and watch the workmen craft this house."

Rebecca followed him. "I wouldn't know. Papa left me in Chicago until the house was finished."

He smoothed a gloved hand along a strip of chair rail molding. "Shame. It was a sight to behold. The men who built this place were artists."

She glanced up the stairs, her nerves stretching tighter by the minute. *Stay upstairs, Bess and Mac.*

"I never would have imagined you'd have turned this place into an inn," he said.

She let her own bitterness show. "My husband didn't leave me much choice."

He stared at a delicate blue-and-white vase sitting on a cherry side table. "Still, with all the money your pa had, I'd figured you'd be fixed for life. Your daddy was a king in these parts."

"My husband took *all* of it."

"So you opened your house up to strangers?"

She blinked at his implied criticism. "Like I said, I didn't have a choice."

He frowned and took a step toward her. He stood so close she could feel the heat of his body. "You ever worry about having strangers sleeping under your own roof? There's no telling what could happen to a woman alone with a small child."

The top of her head barely reached his shoulders, making her feel small and vulnerable. She'd never worried about boarders in her house—until now. "I've never had trouble before."

"Then I'd say you've been lucky."

"I do screen my guests."

"That so?" He sounded amused.

Anger ignited, making her forget her fear. "I don't have to explain myself to you, Mr. McGuire."

"You got a gun?"

"That's none of your business."

"Do you have a gun?" he replied as if talking to a child.

"Yes."

"You know how to use it?"

"It belonged to my father and it's old."

"That mean no or yes?"

Frustration ate at her. "My safety is none of your concern, Mr. McGuire. My son and I got along just fine before you came to town and we'll do just fine after you're gone."

A flash of fire sparked in his eyes. He obviously wasn't used to hearing no. "I'm making you my business."

"I don't want to be your business." She walked to the front door and opened it. "Do us both a favor and leave now, Mr. McGuire."

"Not until I see the gun. I want to make certain you know how to use it."

"I don't want your help."

"Too bad, you've got it." He tossed his hat on a Hepplewhite chair, staking his claim.

She was ready to scream with frustration. Then she heard the squeal of Mac's voice upstairs. "What if I promise to take the gun by to Sheriff Wade later today and have him take a look at it?"

He didn't budge, as immovable as the Rockies. "Better to take care of it now."

His tone brooked no arguments and Rebecca

realized if she were to get rid of him, she'd have to let him look at the gun.

"I keep it under the stairs."

Wordlessly, he watched her walk to a small hatchway and kneel in front of it. She could feel Cole loom over her, waiting.

She reached for the old latch and to her frustration couldn't open it. She shook it, rattled it, but it didn't relent.

Then Cole's strong hand brushed past her. Gloved fingers nimbly flicked up the latch and the door swung open.

"Thanks," she murmured.

"Anytime."

From the darkened alcove she retrieved the double-barreled shotgun, covered in dust and cobwebs. Bits of rust marred the barrel her father had always kept well oiled.

He removed his gloves, tucked them in his belt, and then reached for the gun. His fingers grazed hers. Her skin tingled and burned. She quickly straightened, stepped away and rubbed her palms over her skirt.

He studied the gun with a frown. "You're right. It's old. And in bad shape."

Rebecca felt slightly embarrassed as if the sewing circle had called and found breakfast dishes still in the sink. "It's been in the closet since my father died."

Cole shrugged. "I've got oil in my saddlebag. Once I've bedded down my horse and settled in my room, I'll see to cleaning it right away."

Rebecca willed her hammering heart to slow. He possessed an energy that rattled her senses. "But I thought if I showed you the gun, you'd leave."

"I'll be needing that room now."

Her breath caught in her throat. "Seth's rooms are cheaper."

"I like it here better."

Bess called down the stairs. "Rebecca, everything all right down there? I thought I heard a man's voice." She stopped halfway down the stairs when she caught sight of Cole. "Cole McGuire."

Recognition flickered in his eyes. "Mrs. Gunston," he said softly.

"It's been a long time."

"Yes, ma'am."

She glanced at the shotgun in his hand and then at Rebecca. "What're you doing with that?"

"I suggested Mrs. Taylor keep the gun handy."

"Mr. McGuire was concerned about me accepting strangers into my house," Rebecca said.

Bess grimaced. "I won't deny, I've worried about it a few times, myself."

Rebecca groaned, "Bess, please."

Cole smiled. He had her. "Mrs. Taylor, you should be grateful you haven't had trouble here before. Maybe it is a good thing I'm staying on for a while.''

Bess coughed. "You're staying? *Here?*''

Rebecca shot her friend an overbright smile. "That's right, Mr. McGuire will be needing a room.''

Bess looked as if she'd swallowed castor oil. "How nice.''

The thunder of tiny feet echoed in the upstairs hallway and before either Bess or Rebecca could stop him, Mac appeared at the top of the stairs.

Alert, Cole's gaze shot up, pinning the boy. His expression remained cloaked, but Rebecca sensed he took in every detail about the child. Mac stared back, blatantly curious, then he stuck his thumb in his mouth.

Father and son stood only a dozen feet from each other and neither knew it. Shame rushed through Rebecca even as she prayed Cole didn't sense his connection to Mac.

Bess looked at Rebecca. Her expression screamed, "Tell him". "I thought I'd take Mac for a walk. It's such a pretty day.''

The boy rolled onto his belly and slid backward down the stairs, thumping nosily over each polished wood stair.

Cole moved back, giving the boy extra room to run past him to Rebecca. Mac clung to her skirt

and stared at him. The boy pointed at the shotgun.
"Gun."

The edge of Cole's mouth kicked up. "You
know that guns are dangerous?"

Mac nodded.

Cole knelt down and held the shotgun out. "You
can look at it if you like. Just don't touch it."

Rebecca held Mac back. "I don't want him near
that gun."

"It's best to tell the boy about dangers than to
shield him from them."

Mac looked up at Rebecca. She ran her fingers
through his soft hair. "It's okay, you don't have
to look at it if you don't want to."

The child frowned and turned to look at the gun.
Cole waited patiently, as if he had all the time in
the world. Then the boy released Rebecca's skirt
and ran the distance to Cole.

Rebecca's heart sank. Her son trusted so few
people, yet he'd gone to Cole easily.

Mac touched the gun. "Big gun."

Cole frowned and pulled the gun out of his
reach. "I said don't touch."

"Big gun!" Mac shouted and then without
warning grabbed the barrel. "I want the gun!"

A muscle in Cole's jaw tensed and he rose, un-
folding to his full height. "I said no."

Cole's firm and masculine voice startled Mac.
His bottom lip trembled and he bolted back to Re-

becca. He clung to her and buried his face in the soft folds of her skin.

Rebecca picked him up and hugged him. "You frightened him."

Cole shrugged. "He's gotta understand no means no especially around guns."

"He's just a baby."

"He's old enough to mind."

Anger warmed Rebecca's blood. "I hardly think you're in a position to judge what a two-year-old can or can't do."

"When it comes to guns, I am."

He was right, of course. But it rankled her nerves to have him taking charge, ordering *her* son about.

"I think it's time for that walk now," Bess interjected. She stepped between Cole and Rebecca and took Mac in her arms.

"Good idea," Rebecca said, forcing herself to remain calm. It was more important to put distance between Cole and Mac than give rein to her temper.

Bess paused at the door. "It was good seeing you again, Cole." She shot Rebecca another look of warning then left with the boy.

The high-pitched timbre of Mac's voice blended with Bess's gruff responses as the duo moved through the kitchen. When the back door banged shut, their voices disappeared completely, leaving only an awkward silence between Cole and Rebecca.

"Now about that room..." he said a touch of steel in his voice.

Her head throbbed as she stared at this mountain of a man. How was she going to get rid of him when at each turn he seemed to be digging in deeper?

Resigned, Rebecca knew she wasn't going to win this battle. "If you'll follow me, I'll get your key."

She walked to the library that served as her office. She went to a mahogany secretary equipped with an assortment of cubbies filled with keys. Her fingers shook as she pulled a key out with the number two etched on it.

She turned and gave a sharp gasp. He was right behind her. As silent as a mountain lion, he'd soundlessly trailed her. Unnerved, she stared up at him. He was so close she could see the silver flecks in his green eyes.

He cocked an eyebrow. "That my key?"

His voice broke her trance. "Yes." She held the key out to him. Warm fingers brushed against her skin, sending a shiver through her limbs. "The room's at the top of the stairs. First door on your right."

"You want your money?"

"What?"

"The first night's in advance, right?"

She moistened dried lips. "Of course."

The lines in his face deepened. He dug three silver dollars out of his vest pocket and laid them on the desk.

"Thank you," she murmured.

He walked out into the hallway, scooped up his hat and headed up the staircase. Determined, steady strides shattered the calm silence. His presence filled the house, dominated it.

She hurried to the base of the stairs, gripping the rounded newel of the banister. "How long will you be staying?"

He paused, his foot poised on the top step. "Guess that all depends on you."

Chapter Four

A child's cry woke Cole at ten minutes to six the next morning. He jerked his gun out from under his pillow, cocked it and bolted up straight.

His heart thundered in his chest as he struggled to remember where he was. He studied walls papered in delicate roses, sun-kissed lace curtains, and his own pants hanging over a richly carved bedpost. His mind cleared. He'd taken a room at the Shady Grove Inn.

Rebecca's home.

Cole groaned and eased back the hammer of the gun. His mind drifted back to a night long ago when he'd waited for Rebecca outside this house. It had been the site of a town dance, a party thrown by old man Sinclair to celebrate the town's newfound prosperity. Everyone in town was invited to the dance and Cole had decided to attend.

Rebecca didn't know him, but he knew her. A young girl with blond ringlets and laughing eyes, she came to town only on breaks from school. And when she did he'd steal glimpses of her whenever he could. She was about the prettiest little thing he'd ever seen.

Under the light of a bright moon, Cole had stood on the cold uneven ground as the wind whipped through the trees biting into his coat. Violin music drifted out of the Sinclairs' house and hundreds of tiny candles lined the gravel driveway, lighting the path that led to Rebecca standing on the porch. She wore a silk pink dress and bows to match. Next to her stood her father who sported a dark, smartly tailored suit. Together they laughed easily and greeted everyone with a hearty welcome.

Cole tugged his worn vest down over his lean stomach and stepped from the shadows. He'd worked eighteen hours straight in the mine, but he wasn't tired. He was energized by the promise of a dance with Rebecca.

But as he'd walked into the light, he caught sight of the black grime embedded under his fingernails. Suddenly, his freshly laundered worn denim pants and homespun shirt seemed crude for such a fancy gathering. Ashamed, he balled his fingers into tight fists and drew back into the darkness, anxious she not see him.

He wasn't fit company for her.

And deep in his heart he sensed he never would be.

Cole tried to shake off the old memory as he laid his head back against the down pillow covered in a soft cotton case and squeezed his eyes closed.

The pillow smelled freshly washed and he reckoned was the finest he'd had under his head since he'd splurged on a night in a fancy Saint Louis hotel a few months back.

What had goaded him into staying yesterday? Whatever the reason he knew now it was a mistake.

Hell, hadn't he learned his lesson three years ago?

Three years ago, he'd come back to White Stone, proud of the man he'd become, not to visit his mother's grave, but to see Rebecca. That's when he'd found out she'd eloped with a stranger and was honeymooning in Denver. So, he'd tossed away the dreams of having the woman he'd always wanted but could never have and returned to what he knew: Lily and the army.

Damn it. He didn't belong here—in this bed, this house, this town. And the sooner he left White Stone, the better.

The sound of footsteps padding down the hallway caught his attention. He heard Rebecca's soft voice, couldn't make out the words, but knew by the gentle timbre she was speaking to the boy.

"Mama, Mama."

"I've breakfast to fix but I suppose I could use the help in the kitchen," she said as she passed his closed door.

"Yes. Yes," the child cried.

A moment of jealousy stabbed Cole. He'd never hear his son's voice.

A ghost of a smile touched his lips as he tried to imagine the little fellow. He'd be about two now, nearing Mac's size. Likely he would have stood tall, like Cole. He tried to picture the color of his son's eyes, the texture of his hair and the size of his hands. How long had the boy lived? Where was he buried? Had he cried?

Cole groaned and rolled on his side and tried to stop torturing himself with questions that likely would never be answered.

Angry, he tossed back the covers, stood and strode naked over to his trousers dangling on the bedpost. He reached for the pants, then paused when he got a whiff of horse sweat and campfires. No wonder Rebecca had turned her nose up at him.

Discarding the trousers, he reached in his saddlebag for his spare set of brown britches. They didn't smell much better, but looked more presentable.

Cole dressed quickly. He strapped on his gun belt then retrieved Rebecca's shotgun, now cleaned and oiled, from the top of a wardrobe.

As he strode down the stairs and hallway, Mac's high-pitched squeal echoed from the kitchen. He crept down the hallway, close enough to see, but careful not to be seen.

Rebecca wore a dark-blue dress with a scooped neckline. She'd pulled her hair up into a loose top-knot. Blond curls framed her face.

She had a rag in her hand. Mac sat in his high chair with a mound of mangled hot cakes in front of him. His face was covered with syrup. She leaned forward to wipe the boy's face, but he tried to squirm away.

"Now hold still," she said laughingly. "You look like you've been rolling around in flapjacks."

The boy made a ruckus but when she pulled away the rag he grinned at her. Rebecca's eyes were bright, her smile quick.

The smile transformed her face, erasing the worry lines on her smooth skin as if she didn't have a care in the world.

That was the Rebecca Cole remembered—a happy, young girl, on the verge of womanhood, who always had a quick smile.

He tried to imagine the shape of her legs and the feel of her skin. His body hardened.

Cole took a step back, suddenly uncomfortable. She was beyond his reach now, and always. And there was no sense pretending otherwise.

He tightened his grip around the shotgun's stock, wishing now he'd left town yesterday. He marched into the kitchen.

At the sound of his footsteps, Rebecca stood and turned. Her smile faded and the worry lines returned.

Cole held out the gun. "It's clean. Ready to use now."

She nodded stiffly. "Thanks."

His grip tightened, angry that she still looked down her nose at him. "You know how to use it?"

She stepped back. "Sure."

"Then show me how to load it," he challenged.

"I'll do it later."

He'd be damned if she'd dismiss him. "Get the shells. I'll show you how."

"This isn't necessary."

He wanted Rebecca safe. He didn't know why, but he did and that was all that mattered. "Get the shells."

Rebecca, as if sensing she'd not win this battle of wills, went to a drawer next to the sink, rummaged through the junk stuffed in it, and finally pulled out two shells. She shoved them at him. "Here."

He cocked an eyebrow. "Where's the rest?"

"That's it."

He shook his head. "You're lucky you've never needed this gun before."

"I've done just fine without you or anyone else."

"Like I said, lucky."

He cracked open the gun to expose the empty twin barrels. "Put the shells in yourself so you can get a feel for it."

"Do we have to do this now?"

A bitter smile touched his lips. "Only if you want to get rid of me."

Wordlessly, she stepped up to the gun. Her shoulder touched his as she looked down the twin cylinders. Her lips curved into a delicate frown as she studied the gun. He stared at the creamy white skin of her neck. He savored her closeness, like an opiate. No good would come from his wanting her, but he did just the same.

She inserted the bullets and stepped back. "Happy now?"

Not even close.

He snapped the gun closed. "You know how to pull the trigger?"

"That I do know. Papa showed me."

"Then I'll put this on the top shelf of your pantry. It'll be ready and waiting if you need it."

He went into the closet, stowed the gun on the highest shelf and returned to the kitchen.

Rebecca had pulled Mac from his chair and had perched him on her hip. "Would you like some breakfast?"

He heard the edge to her voice. She wanted him out of her house, but he reckoned years of fancy boarding schools wouldn't let her forget her manners. "No."

"Will you be staying another night?"

If he were a smart man, he'd summon some common sense, ride out of town now and forget all about Rebecca Sinclair Taylor.

Instead, he heard himself say, "Yes," before he turned and left the house.

The sun hung behind a blanket of clouds trying to peek out over the distant string of mountains. Its bright orange light grayed by clouds cast shadows over the miles and miles of sun-baked grass.

Cole headed toward town, not quite sure where he was going or what he'd do.

Farmers bustled about with bushels of produce to sell, blurry-eyed cowhands stumbled out of the Rosebud and women with baskets filled with eggs and jugs of milk gossiped. And they all stopped to stare at him as he passed.

Cole wasn't surprised his presence had upset a few applecarts. He'd ruffled his share of feathers in White Stone. If he'd had a father to keep him in line or if his mother had paid more attention, then maybe things would have been different. But they weren't different, and there was no sense worrying over a past that couldn't be changed.

His boots thumped against the boardwalk and as he strode toward the Rosebud, he heard a young voice yell, "I ain't going back with you!"

"Yes, you are."

Cole stopped and turned to see a burly man grab Dusty by the collar. Fear marred Dusty's face as he squirmed and tried to bite the man's hand. The kid didn't have on shoes and Cole thought his body looked skinnier than it did yesterday.

Passersby gawked at Dusty and the man, but no one seemed interested in helping the boy. The thought stoked Cole's anger.

In five quick strides Cole crossed the street toward the man's wagon piled high with turnip and potato sacks.

Cole recognized the farmer as he got closer. Judd Saunders. He lived about ten miles outside of town where he scraped out a living farming a patch of land. He'd always been known for his mean streak and had never been well liked.

"You bit me, you ungrateful varmint." Judd drew back his fist ready to land a sound punch to Dusty's face.

Cole grabbed Judd's wrist and twisted it behind his back until he squealed and released Dusty. The boy immediately scrambled out of arm's reach.

Judd tried to break free of Cole's grip, but couldn't. He smelled of pigs and sweat and likely, he'd not bathed since last spring. "What the hell is wrong with you, mister?"

"You were about to hit that boy," Cole growled.

Judd's eyes narrowed. "Cole McGuire. Figures you would stick up for a kid like that."

"Stay away from the boy."

"He's my son and I'll hit him if I've a mind to."

The farmer tried to break free, but Cole jerked his arm a notch tighter making him wince. "All the more reason to treat him right."

"He's lazy and good for nothing and I'm trying to teach him the meaning of hard work."

Dusty stepped forward, rubbing his arm. "You worked me in the field twelve hours a day with almost nothing to eat." The heat in the boy's eyes verified the truth of his words.

Cole glared at the farmer. "That true?"

"Nothing's free in this world."

Rage shot through Cole's veins. "Know this. Whatever you do to this boy, I will do to you."

The man snarled. "I don't have to take this from

the likes of a drifter who won't be around much longer.'' He tried to break free of Cole's iron grip, but couldn't.

Cole shoved Judd away easily and watched him stumble and fall on his hands and knees in the dirt road.

Judd scooped up handfuls of dirt and rose to his feet. He faced Cole, snorting like a bull ready to charge, and then threw the dust at Cole's face and lunged.

Cole easily dodged the clumps of dirt and Judd's sloppy advance. He stepped to the side, letting the farmer stumble into a horse trough filled with water coated with a green haze.

Judd reared up his head, murder in his eyes. A semicircle of people had formed around them. Cole noted a few dollars changing hands.

He hadn't meant to start this fight, but he was in it until the finish. "I don't want trouble."

The farmer snarled, baring blackened teeth. "Well, you got it."

Judd came at Cole again, but this time the sound of gunfire stopped him in his tracks. Both men looked to the middle of the street where the sheriff stood, his feet braced apart, a napkin still tucked in his shirt.

Sheriff Wade strode toward them, his blue eyes simmering with anger. "Mind telling me what fight is so important that I'd have to get up from a hot breakfast to come break it up?''

Judd sniffed. ''Just having a little fun, Ernie.''

Cole dusted dirt from his sleeve. ''No trouble, Sheriff.''

Wade stared at the two men, his eyes narrowing. Then he holstered his gun and nodded. ''Take your fun outside of town.''

''Sure,'' Judd said, scooping up his straw hat from the ground.

Sheriff Wade turned on Cole. ''Any more trouble out of you and I'll run you out of town.''

''Fine.''

Cole looked for Dusty, but seeing no sign of him, backed away from the crowd, anxious to be rid of all the onlookers. Only when he was well out of striking distance from Judd did he turn around and set his sights on potter's field. He'd visit Lily and his son's grave and be done with this godforsaken place for good.

He'd not taken five steps when he heard the thud of feet behind him. ''You didn't have to help,'' Dusty's familiar voice called out.''

Cole kept walking. ''You're welcome.''

Dusty hurried to keep pace with Cole's long strides. ''He'll just come back, you know.''

He stopped and glanced down into Dusty's

bruised face. How many times had the boy felt his father's fists? "You okay, kid?"

Dark, untrimmed hair hung over Dusty's blue eyes. A handful of freckles covered the bridge of his nose and his two front teeth looked too big for his mouth.

"Yeah, sure."

Cole grunted. He didn't believe him.

Dusty smoothed dirty hands over tattered overalls. "Hey, you need me to watch your horse today? I got some time on my hands. I reckon Pa's so mad, he won't be back in town for a month."

"Aren't you supposed to be in school?"

Dusty shrugged. "It's a holiday."

"You're a bad liar, kid."

Dusty took two quick steps for every one of Cole's. "Maybe, but I still got the whole day free."

Cole paused at the entrance of the saloon. "When's the last time you ate?"

"Yesterday. Maybe the day before."

"I've a taste for bacon and eggs. Join me."

The boy hesitated. "I ain't supposed to go in there. Mr. Osborne said he'd skin me alive if he ever caught me in the saloon again."

"Why?"

"It might have something to do with missing money."

"You take it?"

"Maybe," the boy said.

The kid was a survivor and if that meant he stole to put food in his belly, Cole wasn't going to pass judgment. He grabbed the kid by the shirt and pulled him inside the saloon. "Keep your hands where I can see them."

The fresh smell of bacon mingled with the stale odor of whiskey, making Cole sorry now he hadn't taken his breakfast at the Shady Grove. He chose a table in the corner. He ordered Dusty to take a chair then took one next to him.

Within minutes Seth sauntered from the back room. His shirt was stained with last night's liquor and his long gray hair hung loose around his shoulders. He studied Cole and Dusty with red-rimmed eyes. "Cole, I'm holding you responsible for anything that boy steals."

"Dusty isn't gonna steal anything." Cole's voice held a threatening note.

Seth reached for a pot of coffee and a pitcher of milk. He set both on their table along with a mug and a glass. "See that he don't. I suppose you'll be wanting breakfast for two." His voice wasn't as gruff as it had been.

"Eggs, bacon and extra helpings of biscuits," Cole said as he poured a glass of milk for Dusty.

"Sure." Seth sauntered to the back room.

Dusty finished his milk just as Cole was raising his mug of coffee to his lips. He poured the boy another glass.

Seth was quick with the biscuits, eggs and bacon. Cole sipped his hot coffee as the boy ate his fill. He marveled at the amount of food the child could pack into his body.

After Dusty had finished his fifth biscuit, Cole chuckled. "Boy, I believe you got a hollow leg."

"Just an empty stomach." Dusty took the remaining three biscuits from the basket and shoved them in his pocket.

"How long you been in town?"

"Pa dropped me off in the spring after ma died. Said I was too much trouble."

Dusty kept all traces of emotion from his face, but Cole noticed the way his little hands shook as he dabbed up the crumbs on the table with his fingertips.

"Why'd he come after you today?"

"Reckon he's thinking about the fall harvest."

Cole felt a hitch in his throat. If he left town now, there'd be no one to look after the boy. Hell, he didn't have anywhere else to be for a couple of months. "I've got some business to attend to, but I want you to meet me here for lunch."

Dusty stood, biscuits bulging from his pants pockets. "You need me to do anything for you?"

"Just show up for lunch."

"Sure thing."

Cole watched the boy scamper out of the saloon, his narrow shoulders a good bit straighter. He swallowed the dregs of his coffee, scooped up his hat and tossed two bits on the table.

He walked over to the bar where Seth stood polishing a glass tumbler. "Where in potter's field are Lily and my son buried?"

Seth stopped what he was doing but didn't look up. "They're not in potter's field. They're in the town cemetery."

"You sure?"

"I'm sure." Seth turned and went into his back room.

For as long as Cole could remember, the town cemetery had been reserved as the final resting place for the town's finest. People like his ma and Lily ended up in crudely marked graves on the north side of town.

Curious now, Cole strode down Main Street past the collection of shops toward a grassy patch of land up on a hill. His boots crunched against the dirt, eating up the half mile of terrain in record time.

He still remembered the cold Friday afternoon in May when he'd stood at his mother's fresh grave. The wind had whipped through the valley that day, blistering his skin as he stared at the plain marker he'd ordered with the name Betty McGuire carved on it.

He remembered how he'd felt—guilty. Guilty that he'd been working when she'd died. Guilty that he hadn't been strong enough to save his ma from the bottle.

He'd barely caught sight of the black iron fence encircling the plots when he saw Rebecca's blond curls dancing in the gentle breeze as she opened the gate that encircled the graves.

He held back, crouching, wondering what she was doing here. He reckoned her pa was buried in the cemetery and maybe even that husband of hers that had got himself shot in Denver. The thought of her pining for a dead husband didn't sit well.

Wicker basket in hand, she knelt in front of a grave. She slipped on a pair of work gloves then carefully cleaned all the fallen leaves and sticks from the plot. She brushed dirt from the headstones then laid a bunch of blue and yellow flowers at the base of the stone marker.

He edged closer, as quiet as the Indian scouts who'd trained him.

"I'm sorry," he heard her say. Her voice sounded strained. Thunderclouds plump with rain loomed over as she covered her face with her hands, chanting, "I'm sorry," over and over again.

His heart constricted at the sight of Rebecca weeping. He didn't have reason to care if she was upset or not, but he did. And when she finally straightened her shoulders and wiped away her tears, relief washed over him.

Rebecca gathered up her basket and rose slowly. Cole backed behind a large tree careful not to be seen.

Wind rustled through the valley. The rusted hinges on the gate groaned as she opened and closed the door, then hurried down the hill, her skirts whipping around her ankles.

Cole waited until Rebecca was out of sight before he rose and dusted himself off, and strode up the hill. He opened the gate, not bothering to close it as he crossed the burial ground. He went straight to the grave where Rebecca had left the fresh spray of flowers.

When he reached the ornate stone marker etched with angels he stopped. His breath caught in his throat and his mind filled with questions.

The name on the marker read: Lily Davis and Child—Never Forgotten.

Chapter Five

Lily, I'm sorry. I'm sorry. I'm sorry.

Rebecca brushed fresh tears from her cheeks as she hurried away from the cemetery down the hill toward town. Leaves swirled around her feet and rain drizzled from gray thunderclouds, ripe and full. Cold raindrops coated her hair and dark shawl.

She tightened her shawl, warding off a sudden chill. She'd been up half the night, unable to sleep as the minutes clicked by slowly one by one. Rebecca had wrestled with the lies she'd told, her mind pulsing with images of Mac, Lily and Cole. This morning she'd risen, blurry-eyed, with a dull headache pounding her head, resolved to visit her dead friend's final resting place.

She'd not been to the graveyard in over two months. Life had become so busy there were always good reasons not to go. But this morning, she'd wanted—needed—to come. She felt compelled to explain her actions and pay homage.

But as she'd knelt in front of the headstone and cleaned away the brush and debris, her gnawing guilt grew worse. It didn't matter that she'd entrusted her own child to Lily's arms, paid for their fancy headstone by selling pieces of her mother's silver or that she'd faithfully tended the grave these last two years. What mattered was that her lies had betrayed Lily's memory.

She stopped her descent sensing someone was watching her. She scanned the rolling hillside as the wind swept over the tall grass. The gate to the cemetery creaked eerily in the breeze, making the skin on the back of her neck tingle. But there was no one.

Feeling the fool, Rebecca resumed her brisk pace down the rocky path. She willed herself to stop crying. It wouldn't do for Cole McGuire to see her like this. He already suspected something wasn't right about her story and if she didn't tread very carefully, he'd discover her secret.

The raindrops fell faster and Rebecca knew if she didn't hurry, she'd be drenched. She ran down the boardwalk, past the drab shops and up the hill toward the Shady Grove. When she reached the front porch gooseflesh puckered her skin and the hem of her dress was damp and stained with mud.

Rebecca took off her shawl, shook the rain droplets from the light wool and draped it over one of the rockers on the front porch. She smoothed a damp curl behind her ear and drew in a deep breath.

She tried to shove her worries aside by mentally detailing what needed to be done for the day. Today was Tuesday. Sheets needed to be washed and floors polished.

As Rebecca reached for the front door it burst open. Dripping wet, Bess stood before her, a bucket full of water in one hand and a scowl on her face. The older woman strode past her and dumped the water over the edge of the porch railing. "The roof's leaking again."

Rebecca groaned. "But I patched it only last month."

"Well, it didn't hold. There's water streaming from the kitchen ceiling and filling up buckets. I don't how in tarnation I'm supposed to cook pies when I got water coming in through the roof. Hell's bells, I finally got Mac down for his nap and now this."

"I'll take a look at it." Rebecca retrieved her damp shawl and wrapped it around her shoulders.

"I don't like you climbing that ladder. You're gonna break your neck if you ain't careful."

"I haven't yet," she said grimly.

Rebecca clutched her shawl and hurried through the pelting rain around the side of the house. She yanked the ladder from under the back porch and dragged it toward the leaky spot in the roof. Summoning all her strength, she tugged on the ladder, straining against its weight and her clothes growing heavier with rainwater. Halfway up, the ladder slipped from her grip and fell crashing down into the mud.

She muttered a curse. If there was money to spare she'd gladly hire someone in town to replace the shingles, but with finances strained she'd hoped to make her roof last until spring. She had to make do.

"I can do this. I can do this."

She braced her mud-caked feet apart then gripped the rungs again and started to pull. Her heart slammed in her chest and her arms burned, but this time she managed to hoist the ladder inch by painful inch up into place, scraping a black gash across the house in the process. Soaked to the bone, she leaned her head against the wood rung to catch her breath.

Recovering, Rebecca retrieved a hammer and nails from the toolbox she kept on the back porch and tucked them in her apron pocket. She looked up the ladder toward the roof. Rain struck her face. Lord, but she hated heights.

She drew in a deep breath and climbed the first rung, and then the second. The ladder shifted in the soft ground and her breath caught in her throat as she waited for it to settle. After tense seconds, she climbed two more rungs. Her foot caught in her muddy hem, forcing her to stop and untangle it.

As she reached for the fifth rung strong hands grabbed her around the waist and plucked her off the ladder as if she weighed little more than a feather.

Rebecca shrieked. Her heart hammered in her chest when her feet touched solid ground. The strong hands whirled her around.

"What are you doing?" Cole's expression was murderous, as he stared down at her, rain dripping from the brim of his black hat.

Anger overruled fear and guilt. "You scared me half to death!"

"That doesn't answer my question."

Her dress weighed down with water, clung to her skin. Her teeth chattered. "I'm fixing the roof."

"Isn't there anyone else who can do that for you?"

"What do you think?" she said tartly.

His face darkened even more. "Give me the hammer."

"Absolutely not, you are a boarder in my house."

"Damn it woman, give me the hammer."

The order was sharp, brooking no argument. She reached in her pocket and pulled out the hammer and nails. "You don't have to do this."

Rough fingers brushed hers as he grabbed the tools from her. For an instant, her icy skin burned. His gaze touched hers and held it a beat longer, before he nodded toward the door. "Go inside."

"I don't want your help." But too tired to argue, she took shelter under the cover of the back porch and watched him expertly scale the ladder. He quickly spotted the loose shingles, righted them and pounded them into place. He accomplished in minutes what would have taken her hours.

A gentle ache settled in her heart. She supposed it was because she'd been alone and struggled for so long, but she couldn't help but wonder if this was the way life was meant to be—a man and a woman working together as partners. Sweet, shimmering emotions swirled inside her as she stared at his broad, powerful shoulders. Foolish to wonder what it felt like to be held in those arms, but here she was standing entertaining romantic thoughts about the one man who could ruin her life.

Cole shinnied down the ladder, then hurried under the cover of the porch. Water dripped from the brim of his hat; his jacket and pants would take hours to dry.

"The patch job will hold for now. When it stops raining, I'll have another look at it. In the meantime, stay off the ladder."

The harsh tone in his voice triggered her defenses. "Thank you," she said bristling.

"You could have fallen and broken your neck."

"Well, so could you!" she retorted.

His lips curled into a bitter smile. "That would suit you just fine, wouldn't it?"

A chill snaked down her spine. As much as she wanted him gone from her life, she'd never will him any harm. "That's not true!"

He snatched his hat off and slapped it against his thigh. "Isn't it?"

She planted her hands on her hips. "You're pushy and overbearing but that doesn't mean I want anything bad to happen to you."

"Liar."

The ground seemed to roll underneath her feet. "What?"

"You said you didn't know Lily very well."

She fumbled to react to the sudden shift in conversation. "I—I only knew her briefly."

He leaned forward until his face was only inches from hers. "Then why leave flowers on her grave?"

She retreated until her back pressed against the door. He advanced. His warm breath brushed her cheek. Her lips trembled as she stared into his green eyes.

"It's right next to Pa's." The excuse sounded lame even to her ears.

"How'd she end up in the town cemetery? Where'd she get that fancy headstone? I can't think of anybody in this town that would have bothered to see a hurdy-gurdy girl buried proper."

All she could do was stare into his angry face afraid to speak even the smallest lie for fear her house of cards would tumble. Cole's gaze bore into hers and she sensed he could almost peek into her mind and read her thoughts.

Then unexpectedly the anger drained from Cole's face and he laid his hands on her shoulders making her jump. The touch of his warm flesh against her skin sent shivers through her body. "We all got things in our past we'd soon forget, Rebecca. I got 'em and I know you do, too. I can see you're storing something inside you and it is eating away at you. Tell me what you know about Lily and my son and I'll forgive whatever lies you've told. I just want to know something about my boy."

The quiet desperation in his voice did nothing

to allay her panic. *You can't have him!* She nearly screamed the words.

Her fear so great, she couldn't bear being so near him. She moved to leave, but he grabbed her by the shoulders and hauled her against his chest.

His eyes searched hers. "You can trust me with the truth."

Trust me. How many times had Curtis said that to her as he bilked more and more money out of this town?

"I can't," she said miserably.

"I'm a man of my word."

"No."

Frustration furrowed his brow. "What aren't you telling me about my boy!" he rasped.

"He's gone," she cried. How much longer could she keep lying? "Please just leave."

He snarled, not listening to her. "I'm not leaving this town until you tell me everything you know."

Hot tears streamed down her face. "I can't help you. Please just leave us be."

He released her and stepped back. "Never."

The back door slammed open. Bess stood there with a fresh bucket of water, her damp hair plastered against her forehead. She glanced at Rebecca and Cole and frowned, then without a word tossed the water over the rail. "The leaking has stopped for now. You two best get inside before you catch your death.''

A humorless smiled touched Cole's lips. He took Rebecca by the arm. ''Bess is right, you're as cold as ice and I don't want anything to happen to you.''

He guided her into the warm kitchen, took her wet shawl from her shivering shoulders and hung it on a peg by the door. ''Bess, Rebecca needs hot tea. She's drenched.''

''I'll take care of her.''

Rebecca shook her head. ''Bess, I'm fine. A change of clothes is all I need.''

Bess snorted. ''You're bluer than a winter sky. If you don't wrestle that chill from your bones you're sure to catch a cold.'' Knowing eyes narrowed as they focused on Cole. ''And you ain't much better. Both of you look like drowned rats. Get your clothes off Cole and I'll wash 'em for you.''

He shrugged off his range coat. ''Not at Mrs. Taylor's prices.''

''No charge,'' Bess said. ''It's the least I can do seeing as you fixed the roof. I gotta say I was relieved to see you scampering up that ladder instead of Rebecca. She ain't got a talent for fixing shingles.''

Rebecca glared at Bess. ''I've managed.''

"Nearly broke your neck last month. You scared ten years off my life."

Cole's jaw tightened. "When the rain stops, I'll get up on the roof and have a look."

"That won't be necessary," Rebecca was quick to say. The last thing she wanted was to be in Cole McGuire's debt.

Cole hung his coat next to Rebecca's shawl. "Seeing as I'll be staying awhile, I'll need something to pass the time."

Bess grinned. "We ain't never had a man around here and we could use the help."

"I don't want a man around," Rebecca snapped.

"You've got one now," Cole said, his words bursting with unspoken meaning.

"Bess, I'll bring my clothes down presently," he said as he strode out of the room, his boots squishing with each step.

"H-he's in-incorrigible," she stammered.

Bess gestured toward Rebecca's soaked dress. "Get over here by the stove and take that dress off. I'll get you a blanket."

Rebecca's fingers trembled as she undid the row of tiny buttons that trailed down between her breasts. More chilled than she realized, she breathed a relieved sigh when she peeled the garment from her shoulders and let it slide over her hips. Her chemise, transparent now, clung to her body like skin. Modesty aside, she stood next to the cookstove and opened the cast-iron door. Her body mopped up the welcome heat as she waited for Bess.

Bess returned in two shakes, a calico patchwork quilt in hand. "Mac's stirring from his morning nap."

"I'll get to him." She wrapped the soft cotton around her shoulders. She shivered.

"He can wait a minute or two more. I want to know what happened outside. Cole McGuire looked like he could spit nails."

"Everything's fine. I've just got to be strong and wait him out."

"*You* wait *him* out? Honey, you're gonna lose that battle. That man had the devil in his eyes. He ain't leaving this place any time soon."

"I will wait him out." Rebecca clutched the folds of the blanket closer together. "Now I have to get upstairs."

Without waiting for Bess's response, she fled up the darkened back staircase. Her bones ached from fatigue and cold. Mac's giggles greeted her when she reached the top landing. She padded across the pine floor to his room and peeked around the door.

Mac sat in the middle of his cot playing with a toy ball. *So innocent.* She wanted to pull him close and savor the feel of his small body against her. If keeping him safe meant damning her own soul, then she'd gladly pay the price.

Rebecca tiptoed away from the door. She guessed she had ten minutes before Mac grew bored with his toys and came looking for her. Just enough time to change her clothes.

She'd go into town today and find Mrs. Applegate. Once she'd assured herself that the women had spread the word about Cole, then she could breathe a sigh of relief. If no one talked, Mac would stay safely with her.

When she turned, Cole was staring at her. He'd moved quiet as a cat in his stocking feet. Wearing dry pants and a worn black cotton shirt, he'd pushed his wet hair from his face with his fingers.

His gaze flickered to her bare shoulder. "You look like you're in a big rush."

"Mac will be up and about soon."

He glanced toward the nursery door where the sound of Mac's giggles trickled out. "Sure."

She moved to step around him. "If you'll excuse me…"

Cole manacled his long fingers around her wrist. His hold was gentle but unbreakable. "I'm not a monster, Rebecca."

She stiffened. "I never said you were."

"You didn't have to. You're just like everyone

else in this town. You hear the name Cole McGuire and your next thought is trouble.''

"No, that's not true." Or at least, it hadn't been until Mac.

A shadow crossed his eyes. "I remember when you first came to White Stone. It was a crisp spring afternoon. Your pa had finished building his house and he'd finally sent for you.''

Rebecca remembered that day. She'd been ten years old and hadn't seen her pa in over six months. She'd been so excited to see him that she'd taken extra care that morning when she'd dressed, making sure the bow of her pinafore was extra crisp. "What does this have to do with anything?''

"I was sitting on the steps outside the saloon,'' Cole said quietly. "Your pa was right anxious to see you and he'd nearly worn a rut in the street for all his pacing. I was green with jealously because my own pa had run off before I was born.''

She didn't speak, too afraid the torrent of emotions inside her would spill free.

"I was angry that you had your pa and I didn't. So, I picked up a rock and tossed it on the rump of a horse standing near you. The bay bucked and kicked up clumps of dirt that splattered your dress. You started to cry and I started to laugh. Do you remember what you said?''

"Yes," she whispered. She thought back to the ruined dress and the tarnished homecoming. "I said you were hateful."

"The instant I saw the misery in your eyes, I knew what I had done was cruel."

She conjured vague images of a gangly boy who never smiled. "I stopped blaming you when I saw where you lived and heard what your mother did. No child should live like that."

He laid his hands on her shoulders. Energy surged through his palms, making her knees turn to mush. "I think you're still judging me for those very reasons. You and everyone else in town see only the boy who got into too many fights and stirred up trouble every chance he got." He captured a stray wet curl that had escaped her chignon. "I'm a different person now."

The truth begged to be told. Was she being unfair to him?

"I've got plans to move to California. I want to stake a claim and put what your pa taught me about mining to good use."

California! It was over a thousand miles of hard traveling away. No. No. No!

Maybe he wasn't trouble. Maybe he could be a father to Mac. But Rebecca couldn't let him take Mac that far away. She pulled away from him. "I wish you the best, Cole, truly."

His jaw tightened. "I'm asking this one last time, Rebecca. Tell me what you know."

Mac cried out to her. "Mama!"

She stared at the nursery door. "I don't know anything." *Have mercy on my soul.*

He grabbed her by the arm, his fingers biting into her skin. He jerked her close to him. "If I find out you've been lying to me, I promise you I will make you pay, Rebecca."

She broke free and fled into the nursery afraid to think or move. Her heart slammed against her chest.

Rebecca had trapped herself with her own lies.

Chapter Six

Cole bit back an oath, scooped up his hat and stormed down the stairs and out the front door. The rain had cleared. The cloudy haze had split to reveal a blue sky. A dewy film clung to the leaves and the streets had turned to a muddy quagmire.

Cole had given Rebecca ample opportunity to tell him what she knew about his boy. Hell, he wasn't asking for much.

Damn Rebecca! He'd gone out of his way to be thoughtful concerning her feelings, but she kept holding back.

Double damn him for caring that she didn't trust him. He smacked his fist against the porch railing.

If he had a lick of sense he'd shake every last grain of truth out of her. But, blast his hide, he did care.

Cole wanted Rebecca to trust him. He wanted

her to recognize him for the man he'd become—a man worthy of her confidence.

But when he looked into her light-blue eyes, he saw only fear and distrust. She was afraid of him and she wasn't going to tell him anything.

Well, by God, there was more than one way to skin a cat. From his pocket he pulled out a battered watch and snapped it open. Ten-fifteen. Dusty wouldn't be meeting him at the Rosebud for nearly two hours, which gave him ample time to start nosing around. If Rebecca wouldn't talk to him, someone else would.

Cole dug his heel into a warped floorboard on the porch. "I tried to be a nice guy, Rebecca."

He put on his hat and strode down the steps toward town. Thick mud caked his boots, but his gait was sure and purposeful. He'd talk to every person in town if that's what it took. And if no one talked, they'd learn that Cole McGuire could stir up a lot more trouble now than he ever did before.

He'd just reached the inn's picket fence when he saw Sheriff Wade striding toward him with Dusty in tow. He held the boy by his collar, forcing him to take three steps for each one of his.

Dusty wore a panicked expression even as he kicked and squirmed each step of the way. "Let me go, I ain't done nothing wrong, Sheriff."

"Hush up, boy. We'll just see what you been up to and ain't." Sheriff Wade's dented tin star caught the sunlight and his round belly jostled as he dragged the boy down the rutted path.

Cole thought back to his own youth. Whenever there'd been a speck of trouble, he had been the one they'd come looking for, whether it was stolen apples or missing money. Wade hadn't been the one looking for him in those days, but that didn't stop him from resenting the man.

Cole stopped at the fence, his hand resting on twin pickets. "What seems to be the problem, Sheriff?"

The old man halted and spat. He wore a clean shirt, had trimmed his beard and the strong smell of bay rum wafted around him.

"You're just the one I'm looking for."

"That so?"

Dusty squirmed against Wade's meaty hold. "Tell him I ain't been looking for trouble," he shouted.

"Hush boy," Wade warned. "Or I'll jerk a knot in you."

Cole's fingers bit into the pickets. "No need to be rough with the boy."

"Rough's about all he understands."

"I'm asking you real polite. Let go of him."

Challenge flashed in the sheriff's old eyes as he

tightened his hold on Dusty. "He's been hanging around the livery. Likely he's looking for trouble."

Dusty wrenched free of the sheriff's grip. The old man lunged toward him, but the boy skirted out of his reach, hopped the fence and took his place behind Cole. "The livery's where I sleep. I weren't doing nothing wrong."

Wade opened the picket fence. "It's high time I took you back to your pa's place."

"I ain't never going back to him again. And you can't make me."

"We'll see about that." Wade strode toward Dusty.

Cole blocked his path. "The boy's my responsibility now. I'll see that he doesn't get into trouble."

"Why would you want to take on the likes of him?"

"All you need to know is that I am."

The sheriff shook his finger in Cole's face. "Just see that he don't get into trouble or I'm coming after you." As if he owned the place, he brushed past Cole, strode across the front yard and up the steps, and knocked on the door.

Dusty moved to run but Cole's arms shot out and he grabbed a fistful of his shirt. "You're not going anywhere."

Dusty grunted. "Let me go."

"No."

Cole ignored the string of curse words the boy spat out as he watched Wade. "What do you suppose that old codger is up to?" He spoke more to himself than Dusty.

"I reckon the sheriff's come courting Miss Rebecca. Everybody knows he's been sweet on her."

Annoyed, Cole glared at Wade's back. "He's too old for her." The vinegar in his voice surprised him.

"He don't think so."

Cole glanced down at the boy's dirt-smudged face. Blue eyes stared up at him with more wisdom than was right for a boy his age. "How would you know?"

"Heard him bragging to the men at the Rosebud the other day that he's got his sights on marrying her."

"She's young enough to be his daughter."

"She's going to the picnic with him."

Cole snorted. The idea of Wade lurking around the inn set his teeth on edge.

The front door of the inn opened then and Rebecca appeared. Bright as a new penny, she'd changed into a dark blue dress and her damp blond curls framed her oval face, she gifted the sheriff with a bright smile. Cole's mood soured.

Dusty poked Cole in the ribs. "You're jealous."

He ripped his gaze off Rebecca to glare at the boy. "Mind your own business."

"Ha! You is sweet on her."

"And you smell bad."

Dusty raised his arm and sniffed his armpit. "I don't."

"When's the last time you took a bath?"

Dusty's face scrunched with indignation. "Ain't been that long."

Cole folded his arms over his chest. "How long?"

"Well, it was chilly outside. April, I reckon."

"That was two months ago."

"Yeah, so?"

Cole took the boy by the arm. "So, it means you're getting a bath today."

Dusty dug his heels in. "I ain't."

Cole pulled him easily along toward the Inn. "You sure are. You smell worse than the sheriff's bay rum."

"Now, that ain't fair."

"Life isn't fair, boy."

Dusty tried to tug his arm free from Cole's grip, but had no success. "What gives you the right to go and toss me in a tub? We was getting along fine and I ain't wronged you."

"Didn't you hear what I said to the sheriff? *I'm* responsible for you now."

A cloud passed in front of the boy's eyes. "Those was just words. I know you were saying 'em to get the sheriff off my back."

Cole stopped and placed his hands on Dusty's shoulders. "Dusty, they weren't just words to me. You're with me now, hell or high water."

His gaze narrowed. "I'm used to being on my own."

"Me, too, but things change."

"Yeah, well, what about Pa?"

"I'll have a talk with him. I'm sure I can make him see reason."

The yearning in Dusty's dirt-smudged face was plain. "I reckon I could tag along with you for a while, but I ain't taking a bath."

"Yes, you are."

The sound of Rebecca's laugh, so clear and bright, floated down to them. He glared up at the porch. She stood close to Wade, too damn close, and was listening intently to something he was saying. The two of them looked as if they were settling in for a nice long visit.

Cole ground his teeth. Why in the devil she would be interested in the likes of a man twice her age was beyond him.

"Boy, it's time you got that bath. And I believe, Miss Rebecca is just the one to help me get you squeaky clean."

* * *

The smell of Wade's bay rum made Rebecca's eyes itch. Her nose wrinkled and she sneezed twice in the first minute of their conversation.

She knew he'd come to talk to her about the picnic. He'd been mooning over her for weeks and so far she'd kept him at arm's distance. He'd been a good friend to her but she'd never had romantic feelings for Sheriff Wade.

Rebecca's nose itched with the thick scent of aftershave. "Turning out to be a lovely day, Sheriff."

He pulled off his hat and clutched it in front of his chest. He'd slicked back his hair and combed his mustache and beard. Deep lines etched the corners of his eyes when he smiled. "Time you started calling me Ernie."

She could feel heat rise in her cheeks. Curtis had been the last man to come courting her and that had been nearly four years ago. She felt wretchedly out of practice.

Rebecca caught sight of Cole striding back up the walkway. Her nerves tightened a notch and she stepped closer to Wade.

Then, she noticed the boy next to him. He was the one who had been stealing pies from her for months now.

Back in April, she'd been hanging laundry on

the other side of the house when he'd snatched a cooling pie. Believing himself hidden, he'd sat down under a shade tree and eaten every bite of the cherry pie. He'd licked the plate clean before carefully replacing the tin back where he'd found it.

Her heart had been overwhelmed with sadness. In him she saw Mac. She wondered who would have cared for her boy if she'd not taken him into her home and heart.

From that day on, she'd made a point to make an extra pie or loaf of bread and set it on the sill to cool. Each time she went into town, she looked for the boy, but so far she'd not been able to get close to him. He was forever scurrying out of her reach like a frightened rabbit.

And now he stood next to Cole. The boy's body was painfully thin; his clothes little more than rags and he wore no shoes. But his eyes were sharp and bright.

Sheriff Wade cleared his throat. "Rebecca, I don't believe you've heard a word I've said."

Startled from her thoughts, she glanced up at him. "Of course, I did."

"Then four o'clock suits?"

"Uh, yes."

He grinned and took her hand in his. "Good. Then it's a date."

"I look forward to it."

"Look forward to what?" Cole asked, a hint of possessiveness in his voice.

Rebecca bristled. "The sheriff and I are attending the picnic together."

His gaze drifted to Ernie then back to her. "When?"

"Next week," she said.

"I'm sure you'll make a fine couple."

Dusty kicked the dirt. "He's too old for her."

Cole nudged the boy, a warning to keep quiet.

The sheriff cleared his throat. "Well, I best get going." Wade faced off with Cole. "McGuire, keep that boy out of trouble."

Cole clamped his hand on Dusty's shoulder. "There'll be no trouble."

Rebecca waited until Sheriff Wade was well past the picket fence before she glanced down at the boy. He stared up with blue eyes, filled with a good bit of false bravado. "What's he talking about?" She kept her tone light for Dusty's sake.

"Dusty's with me now."

"What do you mean, with you?"

"He's going to be bunking with me," Cole said.

"But what about when you leave town?"

His gaze locked on hers. "Who says I'm leaving?"

She ignored the hidden meaning. "You will eventually."

"We'll see." His expression grew serious. "In the meantime, my friend Dusty here needs a bath."

The boy groaned. "I ain't that dirty."

Rebecca had to bite back a smile. She took the child's grimy hand in her own and studied the fingernails encrusted with dirt. The boy desperately needed looking after. "What is it about boys? Mac hates baths, too."

Dusty sniffed. "Who's he?"

"My son," she said tugging him by the hand and leading him toward the kitchen. "He kicks and squirms, especially when I wash his hair."

Dusty shook his head. "You ain't washing my hair."

Cole followed behind. "You're getting scrubbed head to toe."

Rebecca directed Dusty to a seat at the kitchen table. "I'll cut you a piece of cherry pie while the water heats."

A wide grin split Dusty's face. "Cherry's my favorite."

"I thought it might be."

Rebecca made fast work of cutting the pie and pouring a tall glass of milk. She set both in front of Dusty and then pulled a long copper tub from under the sink.

Cole was at her side in an instant. He reached for the tub's sleek edge, his fingers brushing hers. "I'll help."

She glanced sharply up at him. "I'll see to the boy's bath."

His eyes narrowed, as if he weighed the truth of her words. Then he seemed to accept what she'd said and he nodded. "I'll help you."

"Hey! Can I have more pie?" Dusty called out.

Rebecca glanced up to see his mouth smeared with red cherry juice. "Help yourself, Dusty."

The boy grinned, quickly cut another slice and plopped it on his plate. Cherry juice dribbled from the edge of the knife onto the table and the boy dabbed it up with his fingertips, which he licked clean.

Rebecca turned to the sink and pumped cool springwater into a cast-iron pot, but when she turned to carry it to the stove, Cole whisked it from her hands.

"You're taking on a big responsibility with Dusty," she warned.

"I know."

Rebecca lit the stove. An old bitterness crept into her words. "A lot of men walk away from their families without a backward glance."

"Not me," Cole said clearly.

She could feel his gaze boring into her, but she

didn't dare look up. "You don't know the first thing about being a father."

"I'll learn."

Until you get bored or the itch to move on. A retort was on the tip of her tongue, but she swallowed it. It would be foolish to engage Cole McGuire in an argument.

An uneasy silence fell on the room as the water warmed on the stove. Rebecca excused herself to retrieve soap and a towel. When she returned, Cole had filled the tub and coaxed Dusty into the water.

The boy scowled, his arms folded over his chest in silent mutiny. Without his clothes, he looked smaller, like a rain-soaked dog.

Rebecca rolled up her sleeves and knelt by the tub. "Dusty, you look upset."

"I am, ma'am. Ain't natural to bathe."

Cole knelt on the other side of the tub. He had rolled up his sleeves, exposing strong forearms matted with a thick blanket of hair.

Rebecca stared at his long fingers as he dipped them in the water and scooped up a handful of water that he splashed into Dusty's sunken chest. For an instant, the image of those fingers touching her naked flesh flashed in her mind. She caught her breath at the thought, feeling both foolish and strangely alive at the same time.

She focused on the bar of handmade soap in her

hand and dunked it into the water. Building a thick lather, she layered Dusty's dirty skin with it.

Cole's fingers again touched hers when he reached for the soap and she snatched her hand away so quickly she dropped the bar. It plopped into the water and splashed Cole's face.

He wiped the water from his eyes and she mumbled an apology and rose to her feet. "I'll get a pitcher and pour water on his head."

"Ain't I clean enough yet?" Dusty complained.

"No," Rebecca answered as she returned with the pitcher. She dunked the pitcher under the water, filled it, then dumped its contents on Dusty's head. The boy sputtered and cursed a string of words that would shock a seasoned cowhand.

"Boy, don't talk like that when there's a lady present," Cole growled.

Dusty glared at Cole then Rebecca. "She dunked water on my head!"

Cole lathered the boy's wet hair. "Stop your bellyaching. You're nearly fit for company and I don't intend to stop until every speck of dirt is off that body of yours."

A lock of Cole's hair had fallen over his forehead and his eyes gleamed. The gentler expression changed his entire appearance. Her heart softened a fraction, making her wonder again if she'd made the right decision in lying to Cole.

Rebecca ruthlessly shoved aside the doubts and focused on Dusty. Ten minutes later, she dumped the last of the water on him. The bath water was a cloudy gray, but Dusty's skin was a pale pink, and his dark hair had miraculously grown a shade lighter.

Cole held out the towel for Dusty. "Come on, boy, let's get you out of the tub."

Dusty moved to rise but froze when he looked up at Rebecca. His face turned a deep shade of pink. "Ma'am."

Rebecca, accustomed to bathing her child, hesitated and stared at him in confusion.

Cole cleared his throat. "My friend here needs a bit of privacy."

"Oh," she said. She bit back a grin and turned. "Dusty, I laid out clothes for you upstairs in the nursery. They belonged to a boarder who left them behind. They may be a bit big, but they are clean."

Cole cleared his throat. "What do you say, boy?"

"Thank you, ma'am."

"You can turn around now," Cole said.

Rebecca turned to discover Dusty wrapped in a large white towel and his damp hair stuck up. Though he still wore a pained expression, she sensed he enjoyed feeling clean.

A lump formed in her throat. "Go on upstairs."

"Yes'm."

When he was out of earshot, Cole cleared his throat. "I'll pay for the clothes and whatever your costs are for the boy."

"I wouldn't dream of taking your money."

He unrolled his sleeve and fastened the buttons at his wrist. "That's a switch."

"I'm doing this for Dusty's sake, not yours."

"You never struck me as the charitable type."

His words stung. "I would never turn a child away."

"Did you take Lily in, too, when no on else would?"

Rebecca ignored his question. She concentrated on the tub and fished the soap out, not sure enough of herself to look at him. "Dusty's got a good heart," she said changing the subject. "I can see it in his eyes."

Cole frowned as if he understood her ploy. "You're right. But the kid can argue."

Rebecca put the soap in a small bowl on the table. "He's just afraid."

"Like you."

Chapter Seven

Rebecca *was* afraid.

But she faced Cole McGuire to prove to them both that she could handle her fear and him. "I know a frightened child when I see one."

His water-splattered shirt clung to his chest. Eyes the color of jade bored into her. "He's got me now."

The corner of her lips twisted into a bitter smile. "Dusty's been hurt too much. He believes you'll leave at the first sign of trouble."

"I gave him my word I wouldn't."

"Words are easy to spout, even easier to forget."

"You believe I'll leave." The words sounded like an accusation.

She raised her trembling chin. "Yes."

"Like your first husband."

"Yes."

Cole advanced a step. "Don't confuse him with me."

"You two are more alike than you think."

"How?" he demanded.

"You take what you want regardless of who you hurt."

Anger sparked in his eyes. "What have I ever done to you?"

You're trying to take my son! "I don't trust you."

"Why?"

The conversation had taken a dangerous path. "It doesn't matter."

"It does to me." Cole's arm shot out with lightning speed. He manacled his fingers around her wrist. "What have I done to you? You owe me that much."

"Let go of me."

His grip was unbreakable. "Is it because I'm a saloon rat who worked in your father's mines? Is my past so disgusting to you?"

She almost laughed. If only it were that simple. "No."

"Liar. You've been itching for me to leave since the second I rode into White Stone."

"You're here to stir up trouble!"

"I came to find my son. Now, all I want is to

know something—anything—about him. Is it too much to ask the color of his hair? To know if he ever cried.''

"Stop asking me questions. I don't have the answers."

"Lady, you're holding all the cards. And for reasons I may not ever understand, you won't trust me."

Guilt gnawed at her. *I must protect Mac.* "You're not looking for your son. You're looking for a dream, a fresh start."

He released her and stepped back as if her honesty hit a nerve. "Don't pretend to know me."

"You've got this idea of what being a father is about. Yes, being a parent can be wonderful but it is not always fun or easy and sometimes it's just plain hard work."

"I know that," he returned.

"Do you? What are you gonna do when you hit your first hard patch? Leave?" She waved him away, refusing to see any good in him. "Go before you cause any harm to Dusty or hurt him more than he's already been."

He loomed over her. "I traveled over a thousand miles to find my son. *He* may be lost to me, but how dare you tell me I won't stick with *Dusty* when things get tough."

His hot breath warmed her cheeks. His face was so close the heat of his body beckoned her.

For Mac's sake she wished she could believe him, but she knew if she allowed Cole to work his way into their lives, then left, it could be devastating. "A thousand miles is nothing compared to a lifetime of responsibility."

"I'm not leaving."

"You will."

He cupped her face in his rough hands and stared into her eyes. The contact was jolting. Time slowed to a maddening crawl and the world melted away. There was only the two of them.

She should hate him, but she didn't. All she felt was worry, guilt and longing. The icy loneliness that had encased her heart for so long began to melt. And then suddenly, she knew. She wasn't just protecting Mac and Dusty's heart, but her own as well.

A beat or two more passed, and then he kissed her. The kiss wasn't gentle, but insistent, as if born of a torrent of conflicting emotions. She felt branded.

It had been so long since she'd felt a man's touch and her body, with a will of its own, craved more.

Rebecca splayed her fingers against his chest. His racing heartbeat exploded under her palms.

The dangers momentarily forgotten, she gave reign to all the pent-up emotions locked inside her since her disastrous wedding night with Curtis.

Perilous, yet intoxicating, his touch stirred her womanhood. Lord, but it felt good to be desired and wanted. There'd been so many times in the last few years, that she'd imagined herself growing old before her time, unfulfilled and alone. A soft mew escaped her lips.

Cole tightened his arms around her and pulled her closer. He thrust his tongue into her mouth and she willingly received him, savoring his taste.

Now she knew why women whispered and giggled about making love, and why books and sonnets were written about it.

Madness! Insanity! Both thoughts flashed in her mind even as she gathered bunches of Cole's shirt in her hands. His coarse chest hair brushed her knuckles. For the first time in years, she felt desirable and alluring. Wonderfully alive!

Cole's hand slid up her side and cupped her breast. He coaxed her nipple to a soft peak with his thumb as his other hand pressed into the small of her back and pushed her against his hardness. God help her, but she longed to have him inside her!

The sound of approaching footsteps set the first alarm bell off in her head. At first, she denied anything in the outside world encroached. She didn't want this moment to end.

But Cole pulled away. He shoved his hand through his black hair and cursed.

Separate now, the mists in Rebecca's mind cleared. She pressed the back of her hand to her swollen lips. She felt cold, emotionally naked and very foolish.

"Mama! Mama!" Mac's voice echoed in the hallway as he stormed down the hallway.

Rebecca whirled away from the door, needing a moment to collect her jumbled thoughts. What had come over her? She was ready to give herself to Cole like a soiled dove with no thoughts to the consequences.

She sensed Cole standing behind her—could feel the tension in his body. She wished he would just leave White Stone. Only then could life return to the way it was.

She pulled in two cleansing breaths, forced a smile, and then turned in time to greet her son as he hurried into the kitchen. Bess followed behind him.

Bess paused at the door and stopped. Her knowing eyes settled on Rebecca, taking in her flushed cheeks and mussed hair. Her gaze flickered to Cole who stood stock straight, his hands thrust in his pockets. "Don't mean to interrupt."

Rebecca kept her tone light. "Don't be silly. We were just cleaning up after Dusty's bath."

"Is Dusty that half-naked boy asking for clothes?"

"Yes. He's going to be staying here for a while."

Bess shrugged. "He's that boy that's been running around town?"

"Yes."

"Well, I'd best make a bed for him."

Mac grinned. His blond hair was freshly combed off his face and he wore overalls and a red shirt. "Boy!"

"I expect you to be nice to Dusty," Rebecca said kneeling in front of Mac. She knew Cole watched her every move. "He doesn't have a family and he's going to be staying with us for a while."

The boy laid his hand on his mother's shoulder. Small fingers warmed her skin. Mac's innocent touch calmed her nerves. She laid her hand over her son's and smiled at him.

Her priorities came crashing back into place. Curtis's betrayal had taught her that a man's touch might be intoxicating but ultimately it was unsatisfying, destructive and certainly not worth risking her well-ordered life for.

Mac was her life, not Cole.

Mac touched her cheek with his palm. "Mama, where's the boy sleeping?"

Rebecca smiled. "We'll give him a room of his own for now."

Cole cleared his throat. He pulled three silver dollars out of his pocket and laid them on the side table. "Consider this a down payment on the boy's room and board."

Rebecca rose. "I told you, you don't have to pay."

Fire blazed in his eyes. "I take care of what's mine and from this day forward, Dusty's mine."

"Dusty's not yours. He's got a father who can come and claim him any time he chooses."

"Judd's a poor excuse for a father and I'll be damned if he ever lays a hand on Dusty again."

"He's got the law on his side."

Cole smacked the table. "I don't give a damn about the law."

He scooped up his hat and strode out of the room, his spurs jangling in time with the thud of his boots. The front door opened and closed with a bang.

Bess planted her hands on her hips. "Now what's got his feathers in a dander?"

"I don't know," she lied.

"I'll just bet you don't." Bess took Rebecca's

chin in her hands and turned her face from side to side. "His beard scuffed you up pretty well."

Rebecca pressed her palms to her face, her skin still prickling from his touch. "Bess, don't get the wrong idea."

"Oh, I got plenty of ideas and I don't think any of them are wrong." She shook her head. "Missy, you're playing with fire and you are going to get burned."

"I know what I'm doing."

"You don't even have a clue."

Fifteen minutes later Cole strode toward the mercantile, his temper still simmering from Rebecca's words.

What are you gonna do when you hit your first hard patch? Leave?

He had half a mind to stake a claim right here in White Stone just to prove he had changed—that he could stick it out through tough times.

The smell of her scent—roses and cinnamon—clung to his skin even as he tried to shake off the remnants of their kiss. He couldn't manage the task nor could he rid himself of the lingering notion that one taste of her would never be enough.

Cole muttered an oath. He'd never deny that he wanted her. Hell, his fervent response had been proof enough. But wanting and trusting were two different matters and as much as his body ached for her, he didn't trust her.

The bells on the front door of the mercantile jingled softly when Cole opened and closed it. The smell of tobacco and cider greeted him along with a half-dozen sets of prying eyes. He glanced around the room. The hum of conversation stopped and an unnatural silence descended.

A mother and her towheaded daughter, clad in matching calico, stood by an array of fabric bolts that all looked remarkably similar. Hot color warmed the woman's long narrow face before she grabbed her daughter and hurried out the store.

Gladys Applegate stood by the front counter lined with an assortment of glass jars filled with spices and candies. She was as sour-faced as he remembered and still pulled her hair back so tightly, her eyes slanted. She had gained a fair amount of weight in the last three years but she held her nose as high as a princess who'd just gotten a whiff of a bad smell.

Next to her stood Prudence Weatherby and Olivia Farthing, each in calico and floppy sunbonnets. All three women stared at him in undisguised horror before they recovered and turned their backs to him.

Behind the counter Gene Applegate polished a glass jar. He was a tall man, and his white store apron, smudged with dirt and flour, hugged his round belly.

Cole strode up to the counter. He touched the brim of his hat and nodded to the gaggle of whispering women. "Ladies."

Three jaws dropped. Each stared at him as if he were Lucifer himself.

Mrs. Applegate was the first to recover. She puffed out her large bosom. "Mr. McGuire."

Cole turned to Gene. "I'm in the market for some new clothes."

"We don't offer credit," Mrs. Applegate snapped.

"I pay cash."

Gene glanced nervously at his wife. "We got all kinds of fabric and several sizes of ready-made clothes."

"Ready-made."

"We don't have anything in your size," Mrs. Applegate interjected. "I doubt we can help you."

"We got a few items," Gene said, ignoring his wife. Cole knew Gene didn't care who he was as long as his money was good. "They've been on the shelf a good while but they'll suit." He ignored his wife's angry harrumph and walked around the counter over to a stack of men's denim work pants. The storekeeper's practiced gaze skidded over

Cole's long lean frame. "I'd say you're a thirty-two-inch waist in need of an extralong pants leg."

"That's about right. I'll also take a couple of shirts, too. Those white one's will do."

"Sure." Gene gathered the shirts from a pile stacked next to the pants. "Time was I had more clothes in stock, but with the mine closed, there ain't been the demand for much more than I have."

"What you have is fine."

Mrs. Applegate strode over to them. "How's he gonna pay?"

Gene shrugged. "The wife does have a point. Seeing as you're not staying in town, I can't open an account for you. Cash only."

A bitter taste settled in Cole's mouth. "Everyone's so sure I'm leaving."

"Well, aren't you?" Mrs. Applegate demanded.

"Not anytime soon."

"Well, you can't just loiter around town with nothing to do," Mrs. Applegate spat.

"There ain't nothing to hold you in White Stone, Cole," Gene said more calmly. "There's barely enough work to keep the livery running and the sawmill is operating only four days a week now. If the mine were open, there might be something here for you, but the mine will likely never open again."

Mrs. Applegate folded her arms over her bosom. "Do yourself and all of us a favor and leave."

Cole ignored Mrs. Applegate and stared at Gene. "Why didn't Rebecca ever sell the mine?"

"I imagine she still hopes that one day she'll be able to reopen it. But the truth is, she owes so many back taxes on the place I doubt she could ever raise enough money."

"So the town owns the mine now?"

"I suppose."

"Then why not mine it yourselves?"

"It'll take a good bit of capital to search for a new vein. No one in town's got that kind of money."

An idea flickered in Cole's brain. "The old man always thought the richest veins were deeper in the ground."

"That's the rumor, but no one's been able to see if it's true or not."

"Who would I talk to about buying the mine?"

"You?"

"Yeah, me."

"Well, I suppose, it would be the town council. That would be me, Stan and George Haliwell."

"Arrange a meeting. I want to talk to them."

"Why are you even talking about something that'll never be," Mrs. Applegate mocked. "Cole's got about as much of a chance of opening the mine as I got of going to the moon.''

Gene's gaze skittered to Mrs. Applegate then back to Cole. ''Even if the council agreed to sell, you'd have to come up with the money to pay the taxes and sink a new shaft.''

Gene was right. It would take a lot of money to get the Lucky Star operational—likely his entire savings. And then there was the matter of Rebecca. She wanted him gone from her life. ''Set up the meeting. I've got the money.''

Gene's fingers linked together in front of his fat belly. His eyes sparkled with excitement. ''You really think you can make a go of it?''

''Yes.''

Gene grinned. ''Well then, can I get you anything else? I got some fine boots over here, rifle shells and a host of food supplies for the trail.''

Cole nodded. ''I need clothes for a boy.''

Prudence Weatherby's sudden intake of breath caught his attention. ''Why would you want clothes for a boy?''

Cole pierced the women with his gaze. Prudence jumped and retreated toward the door. The woman backed into a bag of turnips, sending them spilling out on the floor. She glanced down at the turnips rolling on the floor then back at Cole, as if torn between cleaning up the mess and leaving. She chose to leave.

Mrs. Applegate touched the lace-trimmed collar of her dress. "What size do you need?"

"I don't know exactly. They're for Dusty. Have you seen him around town?"

She snorted. "Who could miss him? He's forever getting in trouble. Why do you want clothes for him?"

"He needs 'em."

"He's got a father to take care of him."

Cole reached in his pocket and withdrew a handful of rumpled bills. "About those clothes…"

She glanced at the money, then pulled out two sets of boy's pants and shirts to match. "Course it stands to reason the two of you would take to each other. Both of you have a taste for trouble."

"Gladys," Gene shouted. "That's enough out of you."

She cocked an eyebrow. "It's true. Let's face it, once a bad seed, always a bad seed."

Gene grabbed his wife by the arm and directed her toward the counter. "Ring up his purchases."

"Don't you order me about, *Mr.* Applegate."

"If this man has got the money to open the Lucky Star he could be the answer to all our prayers."

"I'm simply speaking my mind."

"Gladys, do us all a favor and for once keep your thoughts to yourself," Gene said, a long-suffering tone in his voice. "Mr. McGuire, I'll set that meeting up for you. Come back by here in two hours."

"I'll do it."

Cole turned from the two, shutting out their argument. When he'd first mentioned the Lucky Star, it had been a fleeting idea. But as he turned the idea over in his mind, it started to take root. He had just about as much chance of striking it rich with the claim in California as the Lucky Star.

And the Lucky Star had the added bonus of showing everybody in White Stone—including Rebecca—that he'd made good.

Chapter Eight

Bang, bang, bang.

Rebecca jumped and nicked her thumb with the paring knife. She dropped the half-peeled apple in her hand as droplets of blood dripped from the tiny puncture in her thumb. She glanced down at the large pile of green apples and muttered an oath. Tomorrow's order would never be finished in time.

Bang, bang, bang.

The day was crystal clear, giving Cole the perfect excuse to start repairs on her roof. He'd been up there the better part of the morning, hammering new shingles into place. And for hours all she'd been able to picture was Cole—shirtless, with his powerful legs straddling the roof as he wielded his hammer. What the devil was wrong with her?

She wiped the blood from her thumb and cursed her foolishness. She had more work than she could handle and here she was daydreaming like a schoolgirl.

Cole had been at the inn six days now and he and Rebecca had settled into an uneasy truce. He spent most of his days in town while she tended to the children and to three guests who'd stayed the last two nights.

She didn't know where Cole went or what he did, but he had come to the inn each day for lunch and dinner energized, more comfortable with the town, and showing no signs of leaving.

What worried her most was that she anticipated his arrival each day. When she'd see him striding up the walkway, fear, relief and joy all collided in her. Each time, she'd have to calm her frayed nerves and return to her chores.

Giggles echoed from the corner and Rebecca looked up. Dusty and Mac played jacks. Mac followed Dusty everywhere now, begging endlessly to play. She was certain Dusty would have shooed Mac away by now, but he hadn't uttered the first complaint. He seemed to enjoy Mac's constant chatter.

Dusty's skin was rosier and auburn highlights sparkled from his clean hair. The white shirt Cole had bought for him was already covered in dirt but it, along with the new pants, socks and brown leather shoes, fit well.

There'd been no sign of Judd and the child relaxed more and more each day.

Cole spent hours with Dusty walking down to Miller's Pond to toss rocks, splitting firewood or riding horses. Dusty looked forward to their outings.

Mac had lost his fear of Cole and had begged to be included. So far, Rebecca had successfully distracted him each time he'd asked, but her task got harder every day Cole remained.

She'd not realized until this last week how much Mac needed a male role model. He still favored Rebecca when he was tired, but most times he wanted to play with Cole and Dusty.

Guilt plagued Rebecca as she stared at her young son. He had a right to a father.

Bang, bang, bang.

She sucked in an unsteady breath and prayed their lives would return to normal as soon as Cole left.

And yet, the idea of Cole's departure did not comfort her as it once had. Dusty would be crushed when Cole left and she had grown accustomed to hearing his purposeful footsteps and deep voice in the house.

Mac's head shot up. "Mama, I'm hungry."

Dusty's eyes lit up. "My stomach's growling like a bear."

Rebecca chuckled. "Lunch is only a half hour away. A snack will spoil your lunch."

"Not mine," Dusty said, crossing his arms over his chest like Cole did. "I can always eat."

Mac copied Dusty. "Me, too."

She nodded toward a gray square tin on the counter. "I've got cookies in the jar. Dusty, give Mac a cookie and keep a few for yourself."

He scrambled to his feet. "I'll dish 'em out."

"How about a cherry red peppermint stick instead?" The sheriff's voice surprised them all as it boomed from the other side of the screened door. Hinges squeaked when he strode into the kitchen.

The sheriff had donned a pair of red suspenders, stretched taught over his fat belly. Again the heavy smell of bay rum shrouded the room.

Mac jumped up and down shouting "Candy! Candy!"

Dusty paused by the cookie tin. Talkative with Rebecca, Cole and Mac, the boy remained quiet around others.

She took off her apron and wiped her hands. "It's all right, Dusty."

Dusty didn't move.

Rebecca took the candy from Sheriff Wade. "Thanks. That's very kind of you."

She handed the pieces to Dusty who reluctantly

accepted them. He backed away from the sheriff then returned to his game.

Sheriff Wade hooked his thumbs in his suspenders. "Sure is a distrustful little fellow."

Her eyes softened as she watched the boy give his candy to Mac. "He's got reason."

Mac held his candy up in the air. He squealed with delight. "Candy!" He danced in circles shouting.

The sheriff winced. "He always that noisy?"

Rebecca settled Mac down. "He is a handful at times."

"Likely just needs a man's guidance."

The comment made Rebecca pause but she said nothing. She picked up her paring knife and began peeling more apples.

The sheriff took the seat across from her and made himself comfortable. "You remind me of Dusty."

She stiffened. "What makes you say that?"

"You never take anything from me."

"Of course I do."

"I been offering my help to you for a good six months now and you say no each time."

"But I don't need any help, Sheriff."

"Call me Ernie."

"Ernie," she said testing the name. It sounded awkward.

He smiled, satisfied. "I was surprised to see McGuire fixing the shingles."

"I didn't want him to. He's just taken over."

The sheriff frowned. "I don't like the way he's moving in on your life."

"I can handle him." *I hope.*

"You may know some of the goings on between a man and a woman, but you ain't wise to the ways of men. I don't like the way he looks at you."

The thought of Cole staring at her titillated her. Foolish. Dangerous. "How does he look at me?"

"Like he ain't eaten in three weeks and you're a choice cut of freshly grilled steak."

"Oh."

Mac jumped to his feet and ran to Wade. The boy laid his half-eaten piece of candy in the sheriff's meaty palm.

Wade stared down at the candy. "Thanks, I think."

"Mac, we can't play if you keep running away," Dusty complained.

Mac giggled and ran back.

Wade frowned at the gooey mess on his palm. "Cute."

Rebecca took the candy and handed him a damp rag. "Sorry, Ernie."

Wade wiped his hand clean.

"When I was a young man, children didn't seem to be so loud or so full of surprises."

She laughed. "They have a way of wearing me down at times."

He glanced at the children, then said in a lower voice, "Do you really think it's wise to have McGuire around? It ain't exactly proper."

"He's a boarder."

"Who's staying mighty long."

"I've had other boarders stay longer."

"Ain't the same." He reached in his pocket and pulled out a cigar. "We all figured he'd have been gone by now."

"I did, too." She brushed a bit of flour from her sleeve. "I'd prefer you not smoke around the children."

He hesitated as if he were going to argue then put the cigar back in his pocket. "Whatever you say."

"Mr. McGuire will leave soon."

Wade laid his warm, damp hand over hers. "What're you gonna do if Cole stays for good?"

Panic flared. Hope blossomed. "He won't."

"I hear he was talking to the mayor and a handful of others. No one's talking, which ain't like any of them."

"What do you think they're talking about?"

"Can't say. But I reckon it's big."

"Maybe he asked him to leave town."

"Don't think so. I saw Gene shake his hand yesterday. They was thick as thieves."

Until now, she *had* expected him to leave White Stone. Now she wasn't so sure. "I can't keep lying forever."

"No." He took her hand in his. "I been thinking about another way to get you out of this mess."

"What's that?"

"Marry me."

Rebecca swallowed wrong and started to cough. A handful of seconds passed before she caught her breath. "What?"

"I know it's sudden for you, but it's just about all I could think about since I first laid eyes on you."

"Ernie, please."

"I don't want your answer now, but give it serious thought. I know I'm as old as your pa, but I've got a mind to settle down and have a family. I'd raise Mac, and Dusty if you want, as my own."

"Oh, my." Her head started spinning. She'd known the sheriff had been interested in her but she had no idea his feelings ran this deep.

"And I'll protect you from Cole. With a husband by your side, no one would take, well…you know."

She tugged her hand free. "Ernie, I need to think about your offer."

The back door squeaked open. "And what offer would that be?" Cole asked, his raspy voice grating on her exposed nerves.

She started. He stood in the doorway. He wore no shirt, his bronzed skin glistening with sweat. Thick hair matted his chest and trailed down to his narrow waist. His hair was tousled by the wind and his eyes blazed with anger. He had wrapped a bandanna around his left hand. Blood stained the rag and his pants.

"It's none of your concern," she said, primly.

"Like hell." He strode into the room, his boots thudding against the wooden floor. Blood dripped from his makeshift bandage.

"You're bleeding," she said, concerned.

"I'll live. What's Wade want?"

Sheriff Wade straightened his shoulders. "If you must know, I've asked Rebecca to marry me."

Cole's gaze darkened. "That so? What'd she say?"

"She's got to think about it," Sheriff Wade said.

"Sudden isn't it, Wade?"

"Not really. We've known each other six months."

Rebecca inhaled sharply. She was starting to feel

like the prize in a tug-of-war match. "*She's* still in the room."

Cole stared mutinously at her.

Wade's cheeks reddened with embarrassment. "Sorry."

Rebecca sighed. "Ernie, would you please leave?"

He hesitated. "Will you promise to consider my offer?"

"Yes."

Wade glared at Cole as he spoke to Rebecca. "You gonna be okay?"

"Yes, yes. I'll be fine."

"All right," he grumbled. "But if you need me for anything, just call."

Rebecca walked him to the back door and opened it. "I shall do that."

Without warning Wade cupped her face in his callused hands and pressed his lips to hers. Shocked, she stood wide-eyed and stock straight, staring into his closed eyes.

Ernie blushed and when he opened his eyes, he looked pleased. He tugged his hat forward and touched the brim. "I'll be seeing you tomorrow, Rebecca."

"Tomorrow?" She resisted the urge to rake the back of her hand over her lips.

"The picnic. You haven't forgotten our plans?"

"N-no," she stammered.

"I'll pick you and the children up at four."

"Yes. Lovely."

"Until then." He nodded and left.

When Rebecca turned three sets of eyes were staring at her. The children didn't hide their shock. Cole didn't hide his anger.

"That's gross," Dusty said.

"Gross," Mac chimed.

Cole winked at the children. "You each get extra candy for that. Dusty, take Mac out back for a minute then I'll run you both down to the mercantile for that candy. I need a word with Miss Rebecca."

"Can I pick any flavor I want?" Dusty asked.

"You can buy out the whole damn store, kid."

"Great!" Dusty shouted.

"Great!" Mac repeated.

Dusty tossed the untouched candy Wade had given him on the table and guided Mac outside. The boys quickly settled into a game of good-guy, bad-guy.

"You're bribing those boys with candy," Rebecca challenged.

He ignored her. "You're not considering marrying that guy, are you?"

"That's none of your business."

Rebecca pretended an indifference she didn't

feel and focused on Cole's bleeding hand. "Let me have a look at your hand?"

He jerked away from her when she reached for the dirty bandanna wrapped around his hand. "Don't change the subject."

"You're bleeding on my floor."

"It's fine."

"I just cleaned this floor and I'd like it to remain presentable for another day or two." She took a hold of his wrist.

He stared down at her, his body rigid, his breathing hot and fast. She didn't speak, couldn't speak. Then relenting, he relaxed a fraction and allowed her to guide him to the sink.

Her stomach flip-flopped as she peeled back the blood-soaked rag, afraid what she might discover. To her relief, the wound wasn't bad. The skin on Cole's thumb was jagged and the thumbnail blue, but the cut wasn't deep. A good washing and a proper bandage would do.

"Did you hit your thumb with the hammer?"

"I was doing fine until *old* Ernie arrived."

"He's not old."

"He could be your grandfather."

"Stop exaggerating."

"I never exaggerate."

"Mind your own business." She pumped water into the sink, letting it splash over the wound.

Cole winced. Rebecca's shoulder brushed his naked skin and she found concentration difficult. She washed the wound thoroughly, then reached for a clean tea towel. "I've got bandages in the closet. Have a seat at the table."

He sat down, leaning back with his legs stretched out and crossed at the ankles. "You can't tell me that you actually enjoyed that kiss."

"It was quite pleasant," she lied. She dug through the basket of torn linens she used as bandages.

"Better than mine?"

She dropped the basket. "Yes."

A slow grin spread across his lips. "Right."

She gripped the handle of the basket to hide her trembling fingers. Careful not to meet his gaze, she took a seat next to him. Her knee brushed his hard thigh. Heat burned in her body.

She swallowed a lump in her throat as she rolled out a neat white strip of fabric. "Lay your hand on the table."

He complied, watching her every move as a hawk did a mouse. "Yes, ma'am."

She smoothed out his clenched fingers. Their roughness brought back memories of him touching her shoulders, her cheek.

She mopped the blood still oozing from the wound with a fresh wad of cloth. Then she pressed more fabric against the gash before wrapping a long thin strip around his thumb, palm and wrist.

Grateful the task was done, she stood ready to make a hasty retreat.

As she rose his good hand reached for her wrist. His gaze was like a caress. She stood frozen unable to react. He drew small circles on the inside of her wrist with his thumb. Slowly, he pulled her down, beckoning her to kneel in front of him. He tugged her closer until each of his thighs pressed against her arms.

"Stop this," she whispered.

"Stop what?" Releasing her wrist, he captured a curl between his fingers.

"Driving me crazy." Her voice sounded hoarse.

"I could say the same for you." He traced the curl along her cheekbone then over her lips. "God help me, but I can't get you out of my mind."

She moistened her lips. "Please, just leave."

"No."

In the next instant, his mouth was on hers. This was no slow, easy kiss like the last. It was demanding, designed to plunder, possess and lay claim to what he thought was his.

A wave of desire shot through her. Ernie's kiss had left her cold. Cole's set her on fire.

She lost herself in the taste of him. His masculine scent enveloped her as easily as his hands. She couldn't resist him, couldn't stop herself from wanting.

She leaned into him, savoring the feel of his muscular chest against her breasts.

A primal growl rumbled in his chest as if he struggled with his own war of resistance. He caressed her mouth with his tongue as his hand slid to her breast. If not for the support of his thighs, she surely would have collapsed. Lord help her, but she sensed her surrender—even anticipated it.

Then suddenly, he tore his mouth away from hers, stood and stepped back. She remained kneeling on the floor, still numbed from their embrace as she looked up at him, spellbound.

The lines around his eyes were deep. He raked his fingers through his black hair. "Let's see if *old* Ernie can beat that." He turned and strode away.

Chapter Nine

The next afternoon the sound of fiddle music drifted to the Shady Grove Inn. A tattered welcome banner hung in the center of town greeting riders and wagonloads of people who'd traveled from all around the county for the picnic.

Cole stood by a pile of freshly split wood near the side of the inn. He had an ax handle in one hand and a thick log balanced on the chopping block, ready to be split. He'd cut nearly a half cord of wood and his muscles ached with fatigue. But the unending restlessness that plagued him remained.

He kept thinking about Rebecca. And touching her. And *wanting* her. After their kiss yesterday, she'd stayed beyond his reach.

She had no business marrying a man like Wade. She was a fool to think he could make her happy.

Cole swung the ax over his head, ready to strike the log when Rebecca and the children gathered on the front steps. They were waiting for Wade to escort them into town.

He lowered the ax blade and set it aside. He tugged off his gloves and flexed his bruised hand.

Rebecca was dressed in a sage-colored dress and she'd swept her golden curls back with a white ribbon. Her cheeks were flushed and her eyes sparkled, with what he guessed was anticipation. She held a large wicker picnic basket in one hand and a parasol in the other.

She looked breathtaking.

Too damn breathtaking.

Rebecca set her basket and parasol aside and knelt in front of Mac to brush his bangs off his little face and tuck in his shirt. Turning to Dusty, she wet the tip of her finger with her tongue and wiped a smudge from his face. Dusty turned his face away, trying to avoid her primping but Rebecca got the spot she was after.

She smiled at the boys. "You both look very handsome today."

Dusty stamped his feet. "I hate these new shoes," he complained. "They're pinching my toes."

Rebecca pulled on lace gloves. "They fit just

fine. You've just got to get used to having shoes on your feet.''

"But I never needed them in the summer before.''

She smiled and kissed him on the cheek. "No child of mine is going to run around town without shoes.''

Dusty ducked his head to hide a grin. His complaining was all bluster, for clearly he cherished his new place in Rebecca's family.

Rebecca's family.

Cole had been an outsider all his life, but he was never more aware of it than he was right now. He wasn't a part of Rebecca's family. Seeing her with the children made him yearn for his son all the more.

Wade strode up the front walk, his chest puffed out like a proud peacock. He carried a bunch of wilted columbines in one hand and peppermints in the other. He climbed the front steps and kissed Rebecca on the cheek as if he owned the place.

Rebecca laughed at something Wade said. Her voice was clear, intoxicating. It irritated him that she encouraged the attentions of a man twice her age. But it irked him more that he cared.

Damn.

Why did he care what happened to her? And

why did it matter that this poor excuse for a town was dying?

The whys didn't have answers and likely they never would. The plain truth was that he did care about Rebecca and White Stone.

Two days ago he'd met with Gene Applegate and the other members of the town council. He'd presented the idea of reopening the Lucky Star, reasoning that if they all pooled their capital, they could have the mine reopened in a month.

In the past, none of them would have given him the time of day. But they were desperate to save their town and would make a deal with Lucifer if necessary. They promised him an answer tomorrow.

Mac's childish squalls broke Cole's train of thought. He looked up in time to see Wade hoist the boy up on his shoulders.

Cole swung the ax blade over his head and drove it into the wood with a loud *whack.* The log splintered in two.

Rebecca's head turned at the sound. Their gazes locked. A primal urge welled inside him. *She was his!* He longed to reach out and touch her, to pull her in his arms and savor her scent.

Yesterday, he'd tasted her passion, but instead of feeling satisfied he was ravenous for more. He wanted to strip away her modest dress and see her naked body beneath his. He wanted her to scream his name as he made love to her. He wanted Rebecca!

As if sensing his thoughts, a fine blush colored her cheeks before she looked away. She smoothed unsteady hands over her skirt before she offered a faltering smile to Wade.

Cole tossed the blade aside. Rebecca was always out of his reach.

"You look to me as if you could spit nails." Bess emerged from the back door, dressed in a freshly pressed black dress with a wide-brimmed bonnet. She carried a glass of lemonade in her lace-gloved hands.

Cole accepted the glass without comment and drained its contents. The sour-sweet liquid cut through his thirst and eased the pounding in his head. "Thanks."

"You best get dressed if you're gonna make the picnic in time."

"I'm not going."

"Why not?"

"Not in the mood for a party."

Cole watched Wade, Rebecca and the children start down the hill toward town. He scowled.

Bess's gaze trailed Cole's. "Cagey old coot thinks he wants children," Bess said. "Thinks a younger woman can give him back something he lost long ago.'' A touch of sadness shrouded her words.

"He's welcome to her.'' Cole didn't sound convincing.

"Liar. You've got eyes for Rebecca.''

Cole thrust the glass back in Bess's hand, embarrassed his emotions were so transparent. "I damn well do not.''

"Your problem is that you're too young and proud to admit you've got feelings for her.''

The sheriff pressed another light kiss on Rebecca's cheek. He offered her his arm and she took it. Cole gritted his teeth.

"If you're smart you won't let her slip through your hands.''

"I can't hang on to someone I've never had.''

Bess shook her head. "I think you're a fool but you do what you please. But I ain't too young or proud to go after what I want.'' She handed the empty glass back to Cole and started toward town.

He stared at the glass. He'd felt at a disadvantage ever since he'd returned.

Ten years ago when he'd rode out of town, he'd sworn to make a success of his life. And by God, he had. He'd traveled from Virginia to Mexico, fought renegades and argued with generals. He had gained a reputation as a risk taker and a man who got the job done. He wasn't wealthy, but he'd saved a small fortune from his military pay and he had his sights set on the Lucky Star. He was a success by any man's standards.

And there'd been women—officers' daughters, ladies of quality—who had had an eye for him.

Yet, even the military, promises of California gold or other women could never erase the memory of Rebecca.

Music and the hum of voices floated from town. There'd be dancing and likely Rebecca would be a popular partner. In a town with so few unmarried women, it was a marvel she'd remained unwed these last two years. No doubt she'd be the belle of the party and every eligible bachelor in the territory would have his hands on her today.

His fingers clenched around the glass.

Over his dead body.

The fiddle player struck up a lively tune and the crowds broke off into couples to dance a jig.

Rebecca stood next to Bess and the children, her foot tapping. She felt out of place at the festivities. Like a forgotten china teapot, she had been left in the cupboard too long and now had been dusted off and put back into service.

Three years had passed since she'd attended one of the Fourth of July festivities. She'd stayed cloistered alone in the Shady Grove, not always happy but safe from men like Curtis. Then Cole McGuire had arrived and changed everything. His presence had turned her well-ordered life upside down.

She remembered the day Curtis had arrived in town on the stage as if it were yesterday. He'd worn a fine suit made of rich dark wool and a brocade vest that shimmered in the noonday sun. His lace-trimmed cuffs brushed the tops of smooth hands, accentuating their long lines and grace. He had dark hair, combed back with precision and a fine wide-brimmed hat that shadowed vibrant gray eyes.

He was nothing like the clumsy town suitors. She had been drawn to him from the instant she'd seen him strutting out of the Rosebud.

Curtis had flashed her one of his heart-stopping smiles and lazily made his way over toward her. They'd talked and she danced with him three times, which had sent the gossips' tongues wagging. But Rebecca hadn't cared. He was handsome, and so charming.

He'd said he was a scout for the railroad and that he wanted to make a home in White Stone. As they'd finished their third dance he'd even whispered that he was half in love with her.

And dear Lord, she'd believed all his lies.

But he was a con man. He'd known who she was before she'd first laid eyes on him. Curtis had

had a talent for sniffing out money. He knew her father, the richest man in the district had just passed away, and that she was alone and wealthy.

Thanks to Curtis, she'd learned a lifetime's worth of lessons. But she was no longer a silly girl, hidden from life by an overprotective father, ripe for a man like Curtis.

"Ah, Rebecca," Gladys Applegate called. Behind her stood Olivia and Prudence. Mrs. Applegate glanced quickly from side to side. "I don't see any sign of Mr. McGuire."

Rebecca's stomach clenched. She remembered the way he'd looked at her before she'd left the inn. The raw longing in his eyes had startled and excited her. "I don't think he's coming."

"He has stopped asking questions about his son," Prudence said proudly.

"No one has said a word," Olivia amended.

"He'll forget about the boy soon enough," Mrs. Applegate said. "He's got his own future to think about."

If success was within Rebecca's grasp, then why did she want to weep? "I suppose."

"Rebecca." Cole's clear voice glided over their heads. She stiffened, turning slowly to face him. Her jaw dropped, as she stood with the other three ladies in stunned silence, staring at Cole.

Cole had combed back his dark hair still damp

from his bath. He'd shaved, which had sharpened the jagged planes of his face. Everything about him, from his newly purchased white shirt buttoned up to his throat, to the snug denims to the tips of his rugged boots spoke of power.

The other women stared wide-eyed at Cole.

"Dance with me," he said.

Rebecca shut her mouth. "I've got Mac to watch."

"I'm sure Mrs. Applegate can keep an eye on him for a minute or two."

"I couldn't impose."

Mrs. Applegate's cheeks had taken on a rosy hue. "Of course you could. Dance with him."

"But Ernie is getting me punch."

"He'll find you soon enough," Mrs. Applegate said. "Dance with Cole."

Before she could come up with another excuse or figure out Mrs. Applegate's change of heart, Cole took her hand in his and tugged her through the throng of people. Wade stared at them with his mouth agape, two cups of punch in his hand. Bess was at his side smiling her approval.

Cole pressed his hand into the small of Rebecca's back, guiding her to the grassy area, matted down by the dancers. The fiddlers played a fast-paced reel, but Cole expertly steered Rebecca into the center of the dancers.

The high-stepping jig made it impossible for Rebecca to talk as she concentrated on the dance. Twice she stepped on his toes. Cole led her through the moves.

"Let me lead," he whispered in her ear.

"Easier said than done."

Slowly, she began to relax. It had been so long since she'd danced. It felt good to move, to be held in a man's arms. She felt as if she were sixteen again.

She'd just gotten accustomed to following his lead when the music stopped. But Cole didn't release her. Instead he held her hands in his. Breathless, she looked past him to check on Mac. He was playing happily with two sticks by Mrs. Applegate's feet.

"He's a fine boy," Cole said. His gaze had trailed hers.

Rebecca's defenses slammed into place. "Yes."

"Who's he named for?"

"His full name is Mackenzie Sinclair."

"Mackenzie," Cole repeated, testing the sound of the name. "Where'd you get that name?"

Lily had chosen it. She'd never said why, but she'd wanted her child if it was a boy to bear the name. "I just liked it."

"That was my grandfather's name. Ma spoke of

him from time to time. She'd always said if he'd lived her life would have been so different.''

Rebecca held her breath. For a moment they stood in silence before she said, ''Where did you learn to dance?'' hoping to shift the conversation.

''You don't grow up in saloons without learning a thing or two about dancing.''

''Was it awful growing up there?'' She'd spoken before she'd thought. ''I'm sorry. That's none of my business.''

Cole shrugged. ''Don't be sorry. My childhood wasn't the best, but my ma loved me in her way.''

''I never knew my mother. She died when I was a baby. It was always father and me.''

''Your father was a good man. He treated me fairly. In fact, he was fixing to promote me if I hadn't gotten into that scrape with Stan.''

''Father was going to promote you?''

''Surprised?''

''He just never talked to me about business. Of course, I doubt I'd have been very interested. I was very silly then.''

''You laughed a lot then.''

Before she could speak the music started again. This time the tune was slow and melodic, the kind reserved for married folks.

''Perhaps, we'd better sit this one out,'' she said.

''Not just yet.''

Cole pulled Rebecca close. Her breasts brushed his chest. Her senses on alert, she tried to move away, but he held her prisoner as he guided their bodies in time with the music.

"This isn't proper," she said.

"Stop worrying."

The heat of his body had a drugging effect. Slowly, she stopped resisting him and succumbed to the urge to lay her head against his chest.

His thigh grazed hers as the music drifted over their heads. Her hand rested on his muscular arm. Sandalwood mingled with his masculine scent. She found herself wondering what it would feel like to surrender to him—if only for one night.

Then the music stopped. She realized she was shamelessly clinging to him. And many people stared at them.

Rebecca pulled free of Cole's embrace. How could she have let him hold her so close? "I'd better go," she stammered.

"I'll walk you back."

Cole escorted her back to Mrs. Applegate and the other ladies who stopped whispering when the two approached. Mac sat on the ground in front of them content to play with his sticks.

"Thank you."

"Two dances in a row," Mrs. Applegate

beamed. "Why, folks are gonna start talking about you two."

Rebecca felt the heat rise in her cheeks. She dared not look at Cole. "They're just remembering the last man I danced with and the disastrous effect he had on my life."

"Nonsense," Mrs. Applegate said. "We were just saying what a lovely couple you two make."

Rebecca stared at Mrs. Applegate. "You were?"

"Yes, we were."

Prudence giggled. "Well, it is only natural."

The blood drained from Rebecca's face. "I don't understand, Prudence."

"Well, seeing that Cole's going to buy the mine."

Stillness came over Rebecca. She looked at Cole. "I'll never sell the mine to you."

Cole's jaw tensed. "You owe a lot of back taxes."

She clenched her fingers, her back ramrod straight. "No one would ever force me to pay the taxes. Everyone knows I will open the mine one day." She looked at Mrs. Applegate for support.

"That's for the men on the town council to decide," the other woman said.

Rebecca rocked back on her heels. "Which is a polite way of saying they'd sell the mine from underneath me."

"Yes," Mrs. Applegate said stiffly.

Rebecca took a step back. "My father built this town. If it weren't for him, there'd be no White Stone. How can you do this to me?"

Prudence stepped forward, pursing her lips. "Rebecca, this town is dying."

Rebecca watched the ladies nod their agreement. The mine was her only legacy from her father. "I won't allow this!"

Mrs. Applegate frowned. "It's time you stop being selfish and start being realistic. If the town doesn't foreclose and sell to Cole, there won't be a town in two years. You've had opportunities to sell and you could have married at any time, but you've turned down every eligible man who's tried to court you. Well, you and this town have run out of options. If Cole doesn't get that mine open, we're all doomed."

Mrs. Applegate's words stung, but Rebecca raised her trembling chin. "Mr. McGuire is unreliable! You've all said so yourself."

"That argument is getting old, Rebecca," Cole said behind her.

Fists clenched, she turned on him. "Do you know how much money they are talking about?"

"Yes."

"You couldn't possibly have enough."

"I do."

She looked around at the crowd that had gathered. Gene Applegate. Stan Farthing. Ernie Wade. None looked surprised. "You all knew."

Wade pulled off his hat. "The council voted to sell Cole the mine an hour ago. We was gonna tell you tomorrow."

She picked up Mac. "How could you do this to me, Ernie?"

"It's for the best," he said.

"I thought you were my friend."

"I am."

She whirled away from Wade to address the crowd that had gathered. "We don't even know Cole McGuire."

Cole laid his hand on her shoulder. "After I buy the mine, you and I will have all the time in the world to get acquainted."

Chapter Ten

An hour later, couples square-danced, the men had set up the targets for the shooting contest and the children played kick ball.

Rebecca sat on her quilted blanket under the shade of a tree. Mac lay on his stomach asleep by her side. She'd have left the picnic but Dusty had begged her to stay another hour. He'd looked so happy, she couldn't deny him. He'd gone off with Prudence's son, Jared, to look at the horses in the livery.

Cole had kept his distance, spending most of his time dancing. The women in town, bedazzled by his transformation, had flocked. Each had taken a turn dancing with him. And to Rebecca's annoyance, it stirred jealous feelings.

Everyone was having a wonderful time.

Except Rebecca.

She felt utterly alone, betrayed by the friends whom she'd known the better part of her life. Five days ago, she'd have bet everything that they'd never side with Cole. And she'd have been dead wrong.

Now that they'd struck a deal with Cole, what would stop someone from telling him about Mac? It was a matter of time before the entire truth tumbled out.

A dark shadow fell on her. She looked up to see Cole. He held a plate with two slices of cake. "Can I sit down?"

"No."

Cole sat down next to her and stretched out his long legs over her blanket. "I brought you a peace offering."

"Go away."

Unruffled, he set the plate down. "Have some cake."

"Ernie wouldn't like it."

Laughter sparkled in Cole's eyes. "He's not been near you for the last hour. I think you scared him off."

"I have not."

An awkward silence fell between them and for a time they sat not saying a word. "No one in town wants to see you unhappy. And they wouldn't have sold me the mine if they weren't scared for their own livelihood.''

He was right. But that didn't erase her fear.

Cole laid his hand on Mac's bottom and watched the gentle rise and fall of the boy's back. He stared at the child for a long moment before he said, "You're lucky to have him."

"I know." She choked back tears.

Cole plucked a blade of grass then tossed it aside. "Why don't you trust me? Is my past so awful to you?"

She'd held herself in reserve since the moment they'd met. He knew it and it was becoming a sore point with him. "No."

He was silent, as if mustering patience. "Then don't you think it's time we called a truce?"

Her back stiffened. "I didn't realize we were at war."

"Right." Anger swirled beneath his words. "If you weren't so stubborn we could reopen that mine together. We could do so much more if we were partners."

He touched Mac's silky blond hair and she had to fight the urge to slap his hand away. *He's my child!* "No."

"What do you have against me?" he said, trying to control his temper.

Nothing. Everything. "Just leave me alone."

He muttered a curse. "I'm taking over the mine whether you like it or not. I'm gonna be in your life for a long time so do yourself a favor and make peace with the idea."

Sheriff Wade approached, his hands shoved in his pockets. He was careful not to meet Rebecca's gaze. He looked like a schoolboy facing down his teacher. "The shooting contest is about to begin. Thought you might like to take a crack at it, Cole."

Cole stretched out his long legs. "I don't have my rifle with me so maybe another time."

"I've got an extra rifle," Wade supplied cheerfully.

"You're making it hard to say no."

"Then let's get you registered."

Rebecca folded her arms over her chest. "Go ahead. Mac and I will stay here."

Cole rose, lifted the sleeping child up and nestled him on his shoulder. "We can go together."

Rebecca stood. She ached to rip the boy from Cole's arms, but she kept calm. "Fine."

Cole cocked an eyebrow. "Lead the way, Wade."

Rebecca stayed close to Cole and Mac. She fretted that the boy would awaken and start to cry, but he slept on Cole's shoulder as if he didn't have a care in the world.

Wade led them to the target area where the men

had assembled with their rifles. Most of the townspeople had encircled the contestants.

Wade strode over to a collection of three rifles and chose two then returned. "Take your pick."

Cole shrugged as if he were almost bored. "Either one will do."

Wade chose a well-oiled Colt rifle. "It's in good condition."

Cole studied the wood stock and sleek barrel. "I can see that."

Mac stirred and raised his head. He looked at his father, then at the rifle. "Bad guns." He popped his thumb in his mouth.

Cole smiled. "You remember what I said about them?"

"Don't touch," Mac said.

"Good job, partner."

Rebecca's heart constricted as Cole smiled at Mac. Holding the boy seemed to come naturally to him and clearly the boy was content to be in his arms. Bess came up beside her and squeezed her arm, as if reading her thoughts.

Tears pooled in Rebecca's eyes. She felt as if she were losing her son.

Wade pointed to a row of targets painted on brown paper and staked upright fifty yards away. "Each man gets six shots and his own target," he said loud enough for all to hear. "The one with the most hits on the bull's-eye wins ten silver dollars.''

A murmur of excitement passed through the crowd as the men nodded and lined up at the firing line. Seth Osborne was the first contestant. He fired and reloaded, missing the center but peppering the outer rim of the painted paper circle with six bullets.

The circle of men and women clapped. ''Nice shot, Seth,'' Stan shouted.

Seth sniffed and moved back. ''You don't own a saloon without learning a thing or two about guns.''

Four other men followed in succession each doing well, but none hitting the bull's-eye more than once.

When it was Wade's turn, he turned to Rebecca. ''Kiss for luck.''

Before she could react, Bess stepped in front of her, grabbed Wade's face in her hands and kissed his lips. The women giggled and the men grunted their approval.

Wade's cheeks blazed with shock as he stood stock straight. ''Mrs. Gunston, what was that?''

Bess chuckled. ''Just my way of wishing you good luck.''

Wade cleared his throat. ''Thank you. I think.'' He stared at her several seconds longer as if seeing her for the first time, then turned to face the target. He paused only a second before firing his six shots. He retrieved his target and proudly showed that four bullets had hit the center. His other two shots were only inches from the bull's-eye.

The crowd cheered and Wade grinned broadly. He held up his hand, waving to everyone.

Cole waited for the crowd to quiet before he handed Mac to Rebecca. His arm brushed hers. Rebecca's breath suspended in her throat as she stared into his green eyes.

Cole glanced at Rebecca. "How about a kiss for luck?" he said in a low voice only she could hear.

"You wouldn't dare."

"Don't ever dare me."

He looked for an instant as if he would kiss her but instead removed his black Stetson and handed it to Mac. The little boy stared at the hat, his eyes wide. "Hang on to that for me, partner."

Mac grinned. "Okay."

Rebecca felt a hitch in her chest as her son stared at his father with wide-eyed admiration. She wondered again if she'd made the right decision to keep the two apart.

Cole turned to face the target and raised his rifle. The people around him still talked noisily about Wade's excellent shots. Some had walked away, believing Wade had won the match.

Cole drew in a steadying breath then fired his six shots. A few people turned back as Wade sauntered to the target, which at first glance appeared to have been pierced by a large single hole dead center. "Well, I'll be damned," Wade shouted.

A couple of the men gathered to stare at the target, each murmuring their approval. All six of Cole's shots had hit their mark dead center in the bull's-eye.

Rebecca felt ridiculously proud of Cole and before she thought said, "Congratulations."

He gave her a rakish grin. "Thank you."

He had the power to evoke anger, fear and passion. He'd yanked her from her self-imposed exile. She knew then that she could lose herself to him. And if not for her fears, she would have.

The clang of the fire bell shattered her thoughts.

Stan Farthing ran down the street waving his arms. "Fire. Fire. The livery's on fire!"

A sudden wave of sickness washed over Rebecca. Immediately, she looked for Dusty who was nowhere in sight.

A hush fell over the crowd. Every man, woman and child big enough to tote a bucket, stopped what they were doing and ran toward the blaze.

Rebecca grabbed Cole's arm. "Dusty's in the barn."

Cole's face tightened with worry. He stared at

her only an instant before he reacted. Moving with
the speed of a cougar in flight, he raced down the
street toward the livery. He reached for the front
doors, but the iron fittings were too hot to touch.
He grabbed an ax that lay beside the barn and
pulled the blade over his head, and plowed it into
the lock. Wood cracked and splintered and the lock
popped loose.

The door swung open. Black smoke poured out.
The fire hissed.

Cole tossed the ax aside and disappeared into
the blaze.

"Cole!" Rebecca shouted. She handed Mac to
Bess then ran toward the blaze. The heat stopped
her advance, leaving her unable to help.

Smoke streamed out of the hole as flames licked
the roof of the livery barn. Rebecca heard loud
voices, the frantic ring of the church bell, the thunder of footsteps behind her.

"Where's my Jared?" Prudence shouted.

"Last I saw him, he'd gone to the livery to play
with Dusty," Mrs. Applegate said.

Prudence ran toward the fire, but Rebecca
grabbed her. "You can't go in there."

"My boy's in there!"

"Cole's gone after him. We have to wait."

Seconds clicked by like hours as the men and
women formed a human chain from the water

pump to the fire. With buckets and pails in hand, they began the tedious task of passing bucket after bucket of water toward the fire.

They all knew if the fire wasn't checked the entire town could be destroyed. White Stone had taken too many financial blows in the last two years to survive the devastation of fire.

Water sloshed, the heat of the fire grew, but no one spoke as they worked together to defeat the flames.

Rebecca's breath caught in her throat as she waited for Cole, Dusty and Jared to emerge. She heard herself scream Cole's name. The acrid smell of smoke stung her lungs as she struggled to breathe.

"Has anyone seen the boys?" she heard someone shout.

"No!" another answered.

Prudence wailed and she rocked back and forth, her arms wrapped around her. Rebecca stood by her side sure her own heart would explode in her chest.

Rebecca realized she'd been so selfish. It wasn't right to deny Cole his son or White Stone the chance at prosperity. Guilt weighed heavily on her heart, making it difficult to breathe.

Then and there she made her bargain with God.

If he spared Cole and Dusty, she'd tell Cole the truth about Mac.

"I swear, I'll tell him everything," she mumbled.

The fire cracked and snapped. The roof groaned. More seconds ticked by. They'd all die if they didn't get out of there soon.

Suddenly, a hand and then another emerged through the smoke. Jared. Behind him emerged Dusty. Rebecca broke into a run, ignoring the shouts from behind her. Reaching into the smoke, she grabbed hold of the boys' shirts and pulled with all her strength.

She dragged them away from the barn. Each collapsed into the dirt, their bodies covered with black, oily soot. Jared and Dusty coughed and sputtered, but they were fine.

"Where's Cole?" Rebecca demanded.

"Don't know," Dusty wheezed. "Was right behind me."

Prudence ran through the smoke and grabbed hold of her son. She hugged him close, stroking his head and whimpering his name.

The support beams of the barn now wrapped in fire, groaned. The fire snapped.

A horse stumbled through the door. The panicked whinny of horses tumbled out with the smoke. Two more horses fled out the opening.

"That's all the horses!" someone shouted.

Cole. Cole. Cole.

Rebecca silently chanted his name as she stood with clenched fists. Then Cole stumbled out of the smoke. He collapsed in the barn's doorway, his face and hands blackened with ash. Rebecca ran back toward the building, now in danger of collapsing and grabbed Cole's shirt and tried to yank him free. But he didn't have the strength to move farther and she didn't have the strength to drag him.

Rebecca's eyes watered and her lungs burned. Her fingers dug into the flesh of his upper arm as she pulled again. Still he didn't move.

"Cole, you've got to get up," Rebecca screamed. "Get up!"

Strong arms reached around her and seized Cole by the shoulders. Sheriff Wade. He dragged Cole away from the barn as a portion of the roof collapsed. Hot embers sailed through the air like a burst of fireflies.

With Rebecca following behind, Wade dragged Cole clear of the barn as if he were a sack of flour. "Damn it, Cole," he muttered. "You best not be dead."

The brigade of firefighters, sweating from the heat, retreated back from the blaze. In the next breath, the roof collapsed. When the building settled, the townspeople tossed more water on the dying blaze.

Rebecca dropped to her knees, staring at Cole's soot-covered face. She combed her fingers through his hair, waiting for him to move. "Oh, God, Cole. Wake up."

"I don't think the fire got to him," said Wade. "His lungs got full of smoke, though."

In a blur of unshed tears, she patted his cheeks with the palm of her hand. "Please, Cole, wake up. I'm so sorry. I'm so sorry."

Sucking in a sharp breath, Cole lay on his side and began coughing. Overcome by spasms, his chest heaved up and down. Several minutes passed before he rolled on his back, breathless.

"Are you all right?" Rebecca nodded.

Cole coughed and nodded. "Just give me a minute."

Rebecca rested her head against Cole's chest. "I thought the roof was going to collapse on you." Her tears stained his blackened shirt.

His eyes closed, he lifted his hand and patted her on the back. "I'm no worse for the wear."

A half hour ago, she'd believed that caring for Cole was foolish, dangerous even. Now she realized how afraid she'd been of losing him.

She turned over Cole's hands and inspected his

palms. "Your left hand is burned." To her dismay, her voice trembled.

Cole presented her with a lopsided grin. "Figures. That's the hand I hit with the hammer yesterday."

Tears pooled in her eyes. "This is no time to joke. You could have been killed."

"It sounds like you were worried about me."

"I was."

"Good."

The townspeople had managed to contain the fire, but the livery was a total loss. The flames had nearly receded. Black embers cracked and popped.

"We're lucky no one was hurt," Wade said. His damp shirt was smudged with smoke.

Stan Farthing dragged soot-covered hands through his hair. "All the horses got out."

Wade turned and looked at Dusty and Jared. They stared at him, their eyes wide with fright, their faces and clothes streaked in black ash. "We was all real lucky. If not for that rainstorm yesterday, this whole town could have gone up like tinder."

The boys glanced nervously at each other. "We meant no harm," Dusty said.

Prudence hugged Jared close to her breast. The boy whimpered, grabbed hold of his mother and buried his face in her stomach. "My Jared has never gotten into trouble. That Dusty boy is likely behind the fire.''

Dusty frowned. ''I didn't do nothing. He was the one with the cigar.''

Rebecca rose and took Dusty by the hand. ''Were you smoking in the barn?''

''We was just having a little fun!'' Tears filled his young eyes. ''Jared stole the smoke from Sheriff Wade. We was just gonna light it up and see what it tasted like.''

''Jared doesn't steal,'' Prudence shouted.

Cole sat up. ''Dusty, no smart man smokes around a barn,'' he said his voice deadly calm.

''We thought we'd ground it out good before we went to pet the horses. The next thing we knew fire had started by the door and we couldn't get out.''

Prudence glared at her son. ''Is what he said true?''

''No, Ma,'' Jared said, his eyes brimming with wide-eyed innocence. ''I didn't do nothing.''

Prudence gloated. ''You see my Jared is a good boy. I knew he shouldn't have mixed with the likes of Dusty.''

''It was his idea,'' Dusty insisted.

Rebecca hugged Dusty close. ''I don't care who started it. Don't you realize you could have been killed?''

Bess and Mac pushed through the crowd. Mac broke away from Bess and ran to his mother. "Mama, don't cry."

She knelt down in front of her children. "I won't, baby."

Stan grunted. "This is all fine and good, but my barn is destroyed. There's no way I could ever afford to rebuild. Those boys owe me."

Prudence sniffed. "I'm not paying one nickel. Jared said he didn't do anything and that's good enough for me."

"I don't have any money," Dusty whispered to Rebecca.

"Then I'll go to your Pa," Stan insisted.

Dusty's face paled. "If Pa finds out he's gonna beat the daylights out of me."

Rebecca nestled him at her side. "Mr. Farthing, I don't have cash on hand, but I've still got a few bits of silver that belonged to my mother. I'll sell those and get you your money."

Tears streamed down Dusty's face. "You don't have to do that."

Rebecca brushed the bangs from his forehead. "Of course, I do. Now stop worrying."

"You ain't gonna send me away?"

"Never."

Cole climbed to his feet and stood behind Rebecca. He dug in his pocket and pulled out the sack that held the ten dollars he'd just won. He tossed it to Stan. "That's a down payment. I'll pay the difference in a few days. When you're ready to raise a new barn, call me. I'll drive the first nail."

Stan stared at the leather pouch. "The boy ain't yours. Why you standing up for him?"

"He's my responsibility now. Good or bad."

Rebecca knew then that she'd been wrong to keep Mac's identity a secret from Cole. Father and son deserved to know each other. She'd keep her vow to God and tell him the truth as soon as they got home. "Cole, you don't have to do this."

His jaw was set firm. "Yes, I do."

She leaned into him and rested her head against his shoulder. "Thank you."

Cole wrapped his arm around her shoulders and pulled her close. "Stan, are you willing to accept the settlement?"

The coins clinked in the sack as Stan jingled it in his hand. "I suppose."

Wade cleared his throat. "The other half will come from Jared's ma."

Prudence stomped her foot. "I will not pay."

Wade glared at her. "Dusty has had his scrapes with trouble but your boy ain't as pure as the driven snow, either. You'll match Cole's ten dollars or spend time in jail."

Prudence's jaw dropped. "I won't."

Wade dug his thumbs in his belt loop and puffed out his chest. "You will."

Prudence shook her finger at Rebecca. "This is all her fault."

Wade rolled his eyes. "Miss Rebecca didn't have anything to do with the fire."

"She took that boy into her home."

"An act of Christian kindness," Wade said.

Unhearing, Prudence shook her head. "She's so desperate for a child, she takes in strays from the street."

Gladys Applegate stepped forward. "That's enough out of you, Prudence. It's time to go home and calm our nerves."

But Prudence wouldn't be pacified. "No, it's her fault. We'd be all better off, if she hadn't taken in Dusty or Lily's child."

Chapter Eleven

"*Lily's child?*" Cole faced Rebecca. His gaze hardened. His body grew rigid. "Mac is Lily's child? My child?"

Everyone stood in stunned silence. Only the hiss of the dying fire and the whinny of a horse penetrated the unnatural quiet.

Rebecca scooped Mac up and hugged him close. "Cole, let me explain."

Cole's eyes glittered like shards of glass. "Is he my son?" His voice was a hoarse whisper.

"L-let me explain," she stammered.

"Is he my son?" he shouted.

"Yes, but—"

Cole sliced his hand through the air, silencing her. His gaze shot past her to Mac and he stared at the boy with fresh eyes. Gently, he raised his soot-covered hand to Mac's small face and caressed the soft skin.

Cole held out his hands to Mac who, unmindful of the turmoil, willingly leaned toward him.

Rebecca tried to cling to the boy, but Cole pulled him from her arms. Her throat tightened. The physical separation stirred panic inside her. "I want to hold my son."

Anger clouded Cole's gaze. "He's my son, not yours."

Mac, content to be in Cole's arm, was more interested in the soot covering Cole's face than old lies. "Dirty."

"That's right, partner," Cole said softly, his voice full of emotion. He touched the boy's face, inspected his hands, his body. "We've got a lot of catching up to do."

Rebecca's heart shattered. "I was going to tell you."

Cole's eyes glittered with raw anger. "But you didn't, did you?" He studied the faces of the people around him. Collectively, people stepped back and pretended interest in the ruined livery. "Did the whole town know?"

Tears streamed down Rebecca's face. "Yes."

"All of them lied for you?"

"Yes." She reached out and took Mac's foot in her hand but Cole stepped back, breaking the contact.

Wade laid his arm protectively on Rebecca's

shoulder. "She's done right by the boy, Cole. He couldn't have asked for a better mother."

Cole snorted. "Mac has a right to know his father. I have a right to know him. How could you all lie to me?"

"We thought we was doing right by the boy," Mrs. Applegate said. "You never seemed the kind to settle down and a child needs a steady home."

"I was going to reopen the mine! What the hell more commitment would it have taken to make you happy?"

Mrs. Applegate flinched. "We were hoping you and Rebecca would get together, marry one day. Everyone would have won then."

"He is *my* child, damn you! You had no call to make such a judgment." He glared at Rebecca. "How did you end up with Lily's child—*my child?*"

Rebecca stepped closer to him. "Can't we talk about this in private?"

He jerked away. "The town knows our business so there's no reason to hide anything now. How did you get Mac?"

"Lily came to me when she was pregnant. My husband had just left me and I was expecting as well. She knew I needed money and offered to pay me if I wrote you a letter."

"What happened to her?"

"She stayed on with me at the Shady Grove. Two months after she moved in, she went into labor. She died hours after Mac was born."

He stood silent, absorbing all she said.

"I did everything I could to save her, but there was so much blood. Days earlier I'd lost my baby. My breasts were full of milk and my heart ached from my loss. It seemed only natural to nurse Mac. I promised myself it would only be temporary because I thought you'd come any day. But it felt so right to hold him in my arms and then you never came. After a time, I couldn't imagine my life without Mac."

"So you decided to keep him for yourself."

"He's not my son by birth, but he is in my heart." She pressed her clenched fist to her chest. "I love him."

"Mama," Mac said, grinning at her.

She reached out to him and he leaned forward, ready to return to her arms. Cole held on to him. "He is my son."

Rebecca's arms ached for her child. "You can't just take him away."

Cole turned and started to walk away from the party. "The hell I can't. Come on, Dusty."

Mac started to whimper and squirm. "Mama."

Rebecca followed. Dread tightened her chest. "Where are you going?"

"Back to the Shady Grove."

Hope glimmered. "Then we can talk. Thank God, you're starting to see reason."

Cole kept walking. "The time for talking is over. I'm going to pack bags for me and the boys and then we're leaving."

Her throat burned with tears. "You can't take my son! And this is Dusty's home now."

Mac, sensing his mother's fear, reached out to her. "Mama."

Dusty hurried to keep pace with Cole. "I don't want to leave."

Cole stopped. He shoved out a sigh as he stared into the boy's face pinched with worry. "We have to."

"You don't have to leave," Rebecca wailed.

Mac started to whimper. "Mama."

Cole faced Rebecca. Pain mingled with anger. "If you'd told me the truth, likely I'd have worked out some kind of arrangement with you. But you lied to me. You told me my son was dead. And I will never forgive you for that."

Tears pooled in her eyes. "I did what I thought was best for Mac."

"Thank you for your help, but I'll take over from here." His voice, deadly calm, carried so much force he might as well have been yelling.

"You can't take them!"

"Mama!" Mac cried.

"Yes, I can." With that, he stalked away from her with Mac crying in his arms and Dusty hurrying to keep pace with him.

Cole's mind, full of colliding emotions, couldn't focus. He hugged his crying son close to his chest. Gravel crunched under his boots as he crossed the inn's drive path in quick, purposeful strides.

He was vaguely aware of Rebecca's cries and Dusty's valiant attempt to keep up with his hurried pace as he strode up the front steps of the Shady Grove. But he didn't stop.

Mac squirmed in his arms. "I want Mama!"

"Later, partner."

"Cole what are we gonna do?" Dusty asked. Worry filled his young voice.

"For now, we'll get cleaned up. I need to think a spell."

Think. He didn't know where to begin.

All the years he'd dreamed of a life with Rebecca. He'd never taken his fantasies too seriously, until today when they'd danced and he'd thought that they had a chance. But it had all been a lie.

Cole squeezed Mac closer. The boy felt small in his arms and an overwhelming urge to protect him welled inside him. He knew he'd sacrifice his life for Mac.

He strode with the boys through the door, climbed the stairs and retreated to his room. Unmindful of the soot on his clothes, he sat on the peach-colored quilt smoothed neatly over the brass bed he'd used this last week.

Mac squirmed to get down. Fussing louder he arched his back and tried to slide out of Cole's grasp. "Mama!"

"Hold on, partner. Stay here a bit longer and let me get a look at you." He tried to hold the boy up so he could study his features.

"No!" Mac wailed.

"I'll give you a silver dollar," he said, desperate.

Mac slapped Cole's hand. "No! Mama!"

Cole dug a silver dollar out of his pocket. He held the shiny coin out for the boy to see.

Mac's crying slowed, but his expression remained mutinous. He stuck his thumb in his mouth. "Dollar."

Cole flipped the coin in the air, catching it easily. "It's mighty nice."

A ghost of a smile touched Mac's lips. He tossed the coin again, then pressed it into Mac's meaty little fingers. "Have a look at that, Mac."

The child stared at the silver coin, fascinated by the way it caught the light. He hiccuped. "Money."

"That's right," he said, grateful the child's cries had stopped.

As Mac studied the coin, Cole stared at the boy, marveling. He'd seen the child dozens of times but now he looked at him as if for the first time. Lily's eyes—bright, brown, full of questions stared up at him. He looked at the curve of the boy's lips and the set of his jaw. Masculine pride welled inside him. That was pure McGuire.

How could he have sired such a perfect child?

Cole touched the top of his son's head. Tears welled in his eyes. "I'll do right by you, boy. I swear."

"Coin," Mac said.

"That's right."

Dusty sat next to Cole on the bed, his young mouth drawn tight. "What are you gonna do?"

Cole wrapped his arm around Dusty's narrow shoulders. "Everything's gonna be fine, Dusty. Don't you worry."

Dusty's lip trembled. "That's what Pa said right before he left me in town."

Cole hugged the boys tight. "I'll never desert you or Mac. You can stake your life on that."

Dusty's eyes brimmed with hope and worry. "Are we gonna leave here?"

"Yes."

"I like it here."

Cole sat stiff. "I did, too," he said honestly. "But we can't stay anymore."

"Because of what Miss Rebecca did."

"Yes."

"What if she says she's sorry? Then can we stay?"

"Sorry isn't enough."

Bitterness tightened around his heart. Rebecca had betrayed him and ruined any chance for them. Damn her! If she'd been honest with him it could have been so good.

The inn's front door opened and closed with a bang. Rebecca. Her hurried footsteps clomped up the stairs and down the hallway to his room. After a moment's pause, he heard her soft knock. "Cole, are you in there?"

"Mama!" Mac shouted. The coin clutched in his hand, he jumped off the bed and ran to the door.

Cole scooped him up before he could grab the brass door handle. "Hang on, Mac." He hoisted the boy on his hip and opened the door.

Frantic, Rebecca stared up at him. Wisps of hair had fallen loose from the chignon and framed her tear-streaked face. His gut clenched with sadness at the sight of her, before he ruthlessly subdued the tender emotion.

Rebecca managed a bright smile for Mac. "Hey, big guy. What do you have in your hand?"

"Money," he said, calming at the sight of her.

"You're rich." She met Cole's gaze. "Can we talk, please?"

"About what?"

"About everything." Desperation punctuated her words. "What are you going to do?"

"Pack up the boys and leave."

Her face crumpled. Tears welled in her eyes. "Where are you taking them?"

"California, likely."

Teardrops spilled down her cheeks. "That's so far. Mac won't understand. He doesn't even know you."

"He will in time," he said unable to keep the venom from his voice.

"I'm his mother."

"Lily was his mother."

"I *am* his mother now."

"Mama," Mac said. His bottom lip started to quiver as he squirmed in Cole's arms.

Cole held the child tight. "You can pack a bag for him or I can, it doesn't matter to me."

Her hands shook as she reached out to Mac. "Please, don't do this. Surely, we can come up with an arrangement."

"You were willing to shut me out of my son's life completely."

She winced. "And I will always regret that."

He didn't enjoy seeing her suffer, but she deserved it. She'd tried to steal his son. She'd broken his heart.

"Good." He slammed the door in her face.

Rebecca knew the true meaning of hell.

She sat on Mac's bed, numb and unable to think or move. The air trapped in her lungs bore down on her heart like granite. She was losing her baby.

She glanced down on the floor and saw Mac's blanket lying next to a pile of toys. She lifted the downy soft cotton blanket and rubbed it against her cheek. It held Mac's scent, a sweet blend of milk and his own musk.

"My baby." Rocking, she clutched the blanket to her chest and started to cry again.

Bess found Rebecca then. She went to her and wrapped her arms around Rebecca. "What's he gonna do?"

"He's taking Mac and Dusty away to California."

"California! He can't take them that far away."

Rebecca shook her head. "I've pleaded with him. But he's too angry to listen."

"Then I'll talk to him."

"I don't think it'll do any good."

"Maybe when he cools off, he'll see things in a different light. In the morning, perhaps."

"He's leaving today." It hurt to speak. "I'm supposed to be packing Mac's clothes now."

Bess's face tightened. "I can't believe he's doing this."

"It's like a terrible nightmare."

Bess rose. "I'll talk to Cole."

"I don't think he'll listen."

Her chin trembled. "Well, that ain't gonna stop me from trying."

Rebecca watched Bess leave. When the door closed she heard the older woman knock on Cole's door. Cole's door opened. There was an exchange of words. His door closed. Bess's soft sobs drifted down the hallway.

Rebecca dug her fingernails into her palms.

It was as if she were watching actors on a stage. Any minute she expected intermission and the actors to take their bows. And the horror of it all would be over.

She rose slowly, her knees almost too weak to hold her weight. In a trance, she made her way over to the small wooden chest where she stored Mac's clothes. She swung open the lid and peered inside at the collection of clothes.

An infant's gown caught her eye. She picked up

the white linen nightie, marveling that Mac had ever been so small. Bess had said it was foolish for Rebecca to keep the clothes. After all, the doctor had said she'd likely never have another child, yet she'd clung to the garments and the memories that came with them.

Rebecca had nursed Mac, cared for him through the chicken pox and scarlet fever and now, God help her, she had to give him up.

She clutched the gown to her face. It didn't matter that her heart was breaking. What mattered was Mac. She needed to be strong and pack the things that gave him comfort.

Tears streamed down her cheeks as she pulled out fresh diapers, pants, shirts and socks for her son. Numb, she rose and shoved the items in a cloth bag. She picked up the blanket and hugged it once again. Reluctantly, she pushed it into the bag.

When she dragged herself downstairs, Cole and the boys waited for her. He'd saddled his horse and packed his and Dusty's few belongings into his saddlebags. Mac sat on the saddle, holding on to the pommel. He look so small—just a baby. Dusty held the reigns, standing tall and proud. Worry lines etched his forehead.

Around them stood Gladys and Gene Applegate, Prudence, Seth, Wade and a collection of other people. They all stood silently watching, their expressions grim.

Bess rushed out with a pail stuffed with food and covered with a checkered cloth. Her eyes were puffy and red. "I packed you food for the road."

Cole shook his head. "No, thanks."

Bess started to cry and Wade hugged her to his chest.

Prudence dabbed a handkerchief to her red eyes. "This is all my fault. I'm so sorry."

Gene Applegate stepped past Prudence ignoring her sobs. He hooked his thumbs in his suspenders. "What about the mine? You're still gonna reopen it, aren't you?"

Cole tightened his fist. "No. You're on your own."

"But we need you," Mrs. Applegate protested.

Cole shrugged. "Too bad."

"We'll waive the taxes," Gene said.

"I don't want anything from you or anyone else in this town."

Rebecca pushed past Gene and stepped up to Cole, Mac's bag clutched in her fingers. "Don't do this. We all want you to stay."

His face looked chiseled of granite. "Are those Mac's clothes?"

"Yes."

He reached for the bag, but she clutched it tight.

Their fingers brushed and for an instant their gazes locked. She imagined she saw a hint of pity in his cold green eyes, but it was gone so quickly she was certain she'd imagined it.

Cole McGuire had no heart.

"I've packed his blanket and plenty of diapers. Have you ever changed a diaper?"

"I'll manage."

Her brows knotted. "The blue pants are his favorite and I've packed his white nightshirt. It's stained, but he won't sleep without it."

Cole ripped the bag from her hands.

"If you stayed an extra day or two, I could teach you how to care for him."

"I'll figure it out." He strode over to the horse, tied the bag to his saddle and hoisted himself up behind Mac, then in one clean move he pulled Dusty up behind him.

"Mama!" Mac called.

Dusty sniffed. "Miss Rebecca. I sure am going to miss you."

Rebecca staggered forward. Her fingers grazed Cole's hard leg. Her stomach clenched. There was no one to help her. No one to stop this horrible nightmare. "My boys."

She grabbed ahold of Cole's leg. She stared up into his face silhouetted by the afternoon sun. "Mac hates green beans and he hates the dark.

Make sure someone teaches Dusty his letters. He's smart and a fast learner.''

Cole gripped the reins. ''I'll take it from here.''

''Cole, don't do this,'' she sobbed, praying she'd reach him. ''Please. I'll do anything.''

''Goodbye, Rebecca.'' He kicked his heels into the horse's side, goading him forward.

Rebecca dropped to her knees, unmindful of the dirt and mud staining her dress. The metallic taste of blood filled her mouth. She realized she had bitten her lip so hard, it bled.

Chapter Twelve

The small campfire Cole had built cracked and sputtered as if it couldn't decide whether it should go out or catch. A freshly skinned rabbit, still half-raw, hung on a makeshift spit over the flames. Stars twinkled around thunderclouds and the wind howled.

With Dusty at his side, Cole reclined on an army blanket spread over the hard ground, Mac in his arms. The boy had finally fallen into a light sleep, but the slightest movement startled him awake.

Dusty squatted in front of the fire, his hands stretched toward the flames and a blanket draped over his shoulders. "Maybe, we should go home."

"We're not going back."

Dusty's lips curved down. "I was getting mighty used to sleeping in a bed and eating hot food."

Cole leaned forward and turned the spit. "We've got blankets to keep us warm and we'll have hot food before you know it."

"I'm hungry now."

Cole forced a smile. "You're just gonna have to wait."

Dusty stared at the half-cooked rabbit then grimaced. "It doesn't look like it's gonna taste very good."

"It'll taste just fine," Cole said, annoyed.

"Rebecca's cooking is the best."

At the sound of his mother's name Mac started awake. "I want Mama!"

Tension crept up Cole's back and tightened around the base of his skull like an iron band. "She's not here."

Mac wailed and struggled to get out of Cole's arms. "Mama, Mama, Mama."

Clouds circled the moon, promising rain before daybreak. This night couldn't get much worse.

Dusty sniffed. "Mac's not smelling too good."

"What do you mean?" Cole had been so focused on the boy's crying he'd not noticed his smell. He did now. "Get his bag from my saddlebag. Dig out a diaper."

Dusty grumbled and pushed himself to his feet. He retrieved the bag Rebecca had packed for Mac and dropped it in front of Cole. "Don't expect me to help!"

Cole balanced Mac in one hand and opened the sack with the other. "It can't be that bad."

"Wanna bet?"

Cole pulled out a fresh diaper. "We're a team now, Dusty."

The boy shook his head after getting another whiff of Mac. "Every man for himself."

"Traitor."

Cole laid Mac on the blanket, then wrestled the boy's shoes and pants off. As if approaching a den of snakes, he carefully opened Mac's diaper. His stomach roiled at what he found. "Boy, whatever you do, don't move."

Mac cried louder and started to kick his feet. "Mama!"

Cole grabbed the boy's legs. "Stop moving, boy, or we're gonna have one mess on our hands."

Mac strained against Cole's grip. He screamed louder and his face turned scarlet. "No! No! No!"

Cole cursed. He raised Mac's bottom and snatched out the dirty diaper. He grabbed a fresh cloth and wiped the boy clean even as the child yelled and clenched his bottom tight.

He grabbed a diaper and cursed as he tried to smooth it flat with one hand and hold the boy still with the other. "How about a dollar?"

"Mama!"

Nauseated, Cole tied the ends in loose sloppy knots. He scooped up Mac and held him close as he breathed a sight of relief. Somehow, he'd survived this first ordeal as a father and had managed.

"Miss Rebecca always washes him with soap and water," Dusty said.

Cole grunted. "This will have to do until we get to a town."

Dusty nodded to the soiled diaper. "What are you gonna do with that?"

"Bury it."

"Miss Rebecca washes 'em out."

Cole stared at the bundled dirty diaper. "Like hell."

"You'll run out of diapers in a couple of days if you don't."

"I'll buy new ones." He hoisted Mac up and looked him in the eye. "You feel better now, right partner?"

Mac stuck out his bottom lip. "Mama."

Cole's jaw hardened. Damn Rebecca. She'd done this to them. If only she'd been honest—trusted him—they could all be together at the Shady Grove living as a family.

He wrapped Mac in a blanket and set him down next to Dusty. Reaching for the spit he turned the rabbit, now blackened on the underside from the flames.

Another hour passed before the rabbit was ready to eat. Each time Cole offered Mac a piece, he pushed the dried out bits of flesh away. Dusty complained about the meat's bland taste after he swallowed each mouthful. Cole bit into a chunk of meat that wasn't so charred. It tasted bland and was as chewy as leather.

Just after midnight, Mac, exhausted from his cries, fell asleep in Cole's arms. Cole stared into the flickering flames, his head pounding. Dusty had stopped his tossing and turning and now lay curled by the fire with a horse blanket around him.

Cole's right arm had started to cramp from the weight of Mac's sleeping body. He leaned forward and tried to lay the child on a blanket, but the boy stirred restlessly and started to whimper.

Cole straightened immediately. The last thing he needed was for the boy to start crying again.

Resigned, Cole relaxed against a rock. He stared into his child's troubled face. Sadness touched his heart. ''Lily would have wanted better for you, boy.''

Cole held Mac's small hand against his own. His tiny fingers barely covered his own palm. Everything about the child smacked of a miracle.

If he'd not come to town three years ago and

seen Lily again…if Lily hadn't wanted their child…if Rebecca hadn't nursed him, there'd be no Mac.

Cole smoothed Mac's silky hair off his face, then touched the wrinkle in the middle of his forehead. Even in sleep the boy looked troubled.

Rebecca's brow wrinkled in just the same way when she was worried.

Rebecca.

A coyote howled in the distance and the wind rustled through the trees.

There was no doubt Rebecca loved Mac. Cole remembered the way she'd begged him not to take the boy. Pity stirred in his heart.

He quelled the softer emotion, reminding himself that Rebecca had brought this all on herself.

Mac stirred restlessly in his arms and whimpered, "Mama." Cole rocked the boy until he quieted again.

Managing the two boys alone, journeying to California and getting a job was gonna take everything Cole had in him. He remembered how his own ma had struggled to raise him alone. She'd worked long hours and Cole had missed her desperately during the lonely nights he lay curled in his bed. Every noise and shadow had scared him. Each time she'd left, he'd feared she'd never come back.

Cole didn't want that kind of life for Mac or Dusty.

But that was exactly the kind of life they were headed toward if he remained a father alone with two boys to raise. There were women he could hire to care for them, but the children would never know the kind of love that Rebecca had given them. A mother's love.

Mac woke up, took one look at Cole and started crying. Cole pinched the bridge of his nose. He glanced past the fire's cold embers at Dusty's small frame huddled uncomfortably in a ball on the hard ground.

Both children deserved better than this.

Cole stared up into the black sky and thrust out a ragged sigh.

As much as he hated to admit it, he needed Rebecca.

Cole awoke at first light. His eyes stung and the muscles in his back bunched into tight knots.

He hoisted Mac and himself up. A thousand needles pricked his legs, stiff from sitting in one position all night. He winced and stomped his feet against the cold ground.

Dusty peeked out from under his blanket. Dark circles hung under his eyes. "What time is it?"

Guilt slammed into Cole. Just yesterday the boy

had been freshly scrubbed and dressed in clean clothes. The worry lines that had disappeared under Rebecca's care had returned.

"Time to go home," Cole grumbled.

Dusty yawned and scratched his head. "How long you reckon it's gonna take us to get to California?"

"We're not going to California. We're going back to White Stone."

Dusty's shoulders jerked up straight. "You mean we're going *home!*"

The boy's enthusiasm pricked Cole's pride. "Yes."

"To Miss Rebecca's?"

"Yep."

At the sound of his mother's name, Mac stopped fussing. "Mama."

Dusty jumped to his feet. "Did you hear that, Mac? We're going home!"

Mac pulled his thumb out of his mouth and grinned. "Mama. Home."

Cole scooped up his blankets, rolled them up and tied them with a piece of rawhide.

Dusty gathered the tin cups they'd used the night before and packed them in Cole's saddlebag. Mac scrambled to his feet, grabbed his baby blanket and thrust it at Cole for packing.

Cole took the blanket, his heart filled with love

and sadness. He wanted to scoop his son up in his arms and tell him how much he loved him, but he held back, fearing the boy would start crying again.

Cole had hoped his love was enough to make up for taking the boy from Rebecca, but he'd been wrong. Mac adored Rebecca.

"Thanks, partner."

"Hope she's made pancakes this morning," Dusty said, a dreamy quality in his voice. "They're the best. She's the best."

A retort stung the back of Cole's throat. He had half a mind to tell Dusty that Rebecca wasn't what she seemed. Instead he swallowed the bitterness. Dusty loved Rebecca, and Cole couldn't rob the child of his love when he'd had so little of it in his life.

Within ten minutes the trio was packed and mounted on Cole's horse. As Dusty chatted happily, anxious to get home, Cole slipped into an uneasy silence.

Two hours later they reached White Stone. Tall gray buildings rose from the valley, an island nestled in a sea of mountains. Cole rubbed the stubble on his chin. He couldn't deny a part of him was glad to be back.

They'd barely reached the outskirts of town, when Prudence Weatherby spotted them. She stood by the mercantile with her shopping basket in hand, her mouth agape as Cole guided his horse down the center of town.

He gripped the reins tighter. Just once he'd like to slip into town without anyone noticing.

Prudence hurried to the edge of the boardwalk. "You're back."

"Yep." Cole hugged Mac closer to him and kept his eyes trained ahead.

Several other people noticed Cole and started to gather by the road.

Gene Applegate hurried from his store, wiping flour from his hands onto his apron. "Thank heavens, you've returned. We didn't expect to see you again. You are staying for good, ain't you?"

"We'll see."

A half-dozen people trailed behind Cole, keeping pace with his horse's slow gait. By the time they'd reached the barbershop, another dozen had joined the parade.

Ernie Wade hurried out of the barbershop, his face half-covered with shaving cream. "You're back."

Cole sat straighter. "Looks that way."

Wade's eyes narrowed. "Couldn't go it alone, could you?"

Cole clenched his teeth and ignored Wade. More people followed him now. Children swung their schoolbooks as they skipped along, ladies whispered and giggled, and shopkeepers flipped their Open signs to Closed.

Even under the best of circumstances, Cole hated choking down his pride and admitting he was wrong. Now he was about to do both with the whole town watching.

Rebecca's head pounded and her eyes burned as she stood at the inn's front window staring down the road toward the distant mountains. She still wore the calico she'd chosen for the picnic yesterday. Covered with streaks of black soot, it was now badly wrinkled.

She didn't care. Her mind, numb from a sleepless night and endless tears, still couldn't believe that Mac was gone. Her baby.

A clock ticked softly. The wind blew outside. Yesterday, laughter and the thunder of small footsteps filled the house. Now, the house was so miserably quiet.

Fresh tears welled in her eyes. She'd never get over the loss of Mac. Never.

She stared down the long, deeply rutted road and wondered where Mac was. Was he cold? Hungry? Did he miss her?

Rebecca hugged her arms around her chest. The thought of living out her days without her son was intolerable.

The sun climbed higher, casting an orange-yellow light over the jagged mountains. Rebecca placed her fists against her temples. She couldn't bear the unanswered questions, just as she couldn't bear the silence. She couldn't go on like this. She needed answers.

And in that instant, she knew what she had to do.

She'd find Cole, Mac and Dusty wherever they were. She'd beg Cole's forgiveness, do whatever it took to win his trust. She'd force him to understand why she'd lied about Mac. Somehow.

She whirled around with nervous excitement. Her fingers tingled as blood pumped through her veins. It would take her time to pack. She turned toward the stairs, her mind reeling with a thousand details. She'd lock up the inn, mark it closed for business, and with the little money she had saved under her mattress, set out looking for her children.

Rebecca's foot was poised over the first step when she heard the horse's whinny. Impatient now to be on her way, she turned, ready to send whoever it was away.

She stumbled when she saw Cole, Dusty and Mac. The trio sat atop Cole's black stallion, each looking saddle-weary as if they'd been gone weeks instead of a single night.

Rebecca blinked, fearing her exhausted mind was playing tricks on her.

Behind them stood most of the townspeople, staring at her and waiting for her reaction. She heard the nervous giggles of several women and saw money change hands between two cowhands.

Dusty swung his leg over the saddle and jumped to the ground. He looked up at the house, a wide, toothy grin curving the edges of his mouth. "It sure is good to be back."

His words broke Rebecca's trance and she raced out the door and down the steps and gathered Dusty in her arms, tears filling her swollen eyes.

Mac started to cry, "Mama" and wiggled in Cole's arms. Rebecca kissed Dusty on the cheek and hurried to Cole's horse. She looked up at Mac and Cole, still not quite believing they were truly here. The sun shone behind the two. She was struck by how much Mac looked like his father.

She reached up her hands and Mac slid into them easily. He smelled of campfire and his bottom was soaked, but as she held him, the fragmented pieces of her heart came together. Everything was right again.

He cried, his tears mingling with her own and moistening her cheek. Staring over his head she looked into Cole's eyes. He'd carefully shuttered his expression, but his jaw was clenched.

"Thank you," she sobbed.

He scowled. "We've got some talking to do."

Not even the ominous tone of his voice dampened her high spirits. "Of course."

Cole swung his leg over the saddle and jumped to the ground. He touched Mac's head gently with his hand. "Inside."

"Okay."

They turned to go in the house when Gladys Applegate stepped forward. "Wait just a darn minute, Cole McGuire. I think we've got a right to know what you're doing back in town."

Rebecca glanced up at Cole's profile, so hard and angry. Truth was, she didn't want to be alone with Cole. She still wasn't certain if he'd let Mac stay and she needed all the support she could get. "I know my neighbors well enough to know they'll follow us inside."

Cole's gaze slid over the crowd. He assessed every man and woman, until several folks shifted uneasily and dropped their curious gazes. "They wouldn't dare."

He guided Rebecca, Mac and Dusty inside the front door. As he opened it, Mrs. Applegate stomped forward. "We're gonna find out what happens in there sooner or later."

"Then it'll be later," Cole said as he kicked the door closed.

Rebecca heard Mrs. Applegate's sharp intake of breath before the door slammed shut.

Rebecca led the boys to the kitchen. Her mind raced with thoughts and worries. She lifted Mac into his high chair and pulled a chair out for Dusty at the table.

Cole leaned against the doorjamb, his arms crossed over his chest as he stared at her. His forearms were deeply tanned and muscular. She sensed a change in him, an intensity that had not been there yesterday.

She fought to remain calm, but her hands trembled as she sliced thick sections of bread and generously buttered each before she set a piece down in front of each boy.

What was Cole thinking? She could feel his gaze bore into her. With deliberate slowness, she poured each boy a cup of milk, careful not to spill a drop.

Cole waited until both children started eating. He then strode toward her. She took a step back, unable to quell her worry.

Cole leveled his gaze on her. He glanced at Dusty who was wiping his plate clean with a chunk of bread. "I've decided to stay in White Stone."

Rebecca's heart leaped. "That's wonderful."

Cole's face remained hard. He rubbed the darkened stubble on his chin. "You haven't heard what I have to say."

Worry prickled her flushed skin. "What do you mean?"

"I want to be a father to my son."

"I understand that." Her mouth felt dry as cotton.

"I want to be there every day when he wakes up and I want to put him to bed at night."

Her throat tightened. "I want that, too," she whispered.

"I figured that." Fresh anger filled his eyes. "I wanted to be all he'd ever need. I wanted Mac and Dusty not to want you."

"But they do," she said proudly.

He scowled. "Taking them satisfied my taste for revenge, but it's too hard on them. As much as I can't abide the sight of you, I won't hurt them."

A wrenching sadness gripped her heart. It shouldn't matter what he thought of her, but it did. "What do we do?"

The world slowed to a maddening pace. The clock in the hallway ticked. The boys chatted happily over their meals. The voices of Mrs. Applegate, Prudence and a half-dozen other people drifted in from an open window. Several townspeople openly gawked at them.

Cole muttered an oath. "You can't swing a dead cat in this town without hitting a nosy neighbor."

She willed her shaking knees to relax. "No surprises there."

Cole thrust out a ragged sigh. Black circles marred the flesh under his green eyes. "It's clear we both love the boys," he stated.

She hugged her arms around her chest. "Yes."

"A child needs a mother and a father."

"We can raise the boys together. I know it's unorthodox—two single parents raising children—but we can do it."

He shook his head. "I won't do that. I won't have folks whispering about them."

"We'll love them enough to make them not care."

Lines creased his forehead. "It won't be enough."

She touched his hand, the one she'd bandaged yesterday. She wanted to forge a connection with him. "We can do this."

Venom filled his expression as he yanked his hand away. "If we're going to do this right, then we do it married."

Rebecca's heart kicked against the walls of her chest. She rocked back on her heels. "Married? But I've done fine without a husband up until now."

"We're not playing it your way anymore. We're doing it my way now."

Terror clenched her gut. "You don't even like me."

"I'll manage."

She took a step back. Her defenses slammed into place. "I won't. After Curtis, I swore I'd never marry."

His gaze narrowed. "Not even for Mac?"

Every drop of defiance drained from her. She'd do anything for Mac and he knew it. "You're sentencing yourself to a lifetime of misery."

He shrugged. "Fifteen, sixteen years at the most. By then Dusty will be on his own and Mac will be grown. Then we'll go our separate ways."

His callous manner stung. "We'll make the children miserable."

"We're both adults. We can put our feelings aside and see that they're happy."

Years of endless tension and unspoken anger loomed before her. How could they possibly make the children happy under such circumstances? "Cole, it can't work."

"If it doesn't I'll leave with Mac and Dusty."

"It didn't work this time."

He shook his head. "I learn from my mistakes. Next time I won't wrench him from you. I'll take my time, wait until he's gotten to know me, and then we'll leave."

The knifing pain she'd endured last night returned in a flash. She was trapped.

The back door slammed open. Gene and Gladys Applegate charged into the room. Slightly out of breath, their gazes darted between Rebecca and Cole.

"Did I hear right, you're willing to marry her?" Mrs. Applegate said.

Cole clenched his jaw. "That's right."

Mr. Applegate yanked off his hat. "And you'd stay in town and reopen the mine?"

Cole nodded. "Yep."

Mrs. Applegate clapped her hands. "That's wonderful!"

Rebecca stared at Mrs. Applegate as if she'd lost her mind. "Don't you understand? He hates me."

"Hate. Love. There's a fine line between the two," Mrs. Applegate said cheerily.

Rebecca stared into Cole's eyes, now calm as if he'd made his decision and was ready to act.

Cole looked past her to Mrs. Applegate. "There a minister in town?"

She nodded. "The circuit judge arrived last night, but he's fixing to leave in a few hours."

"I just need him for five minutes."

Rebecca felt the walls closing in on her. She glanced at the door. "I need to be alone to think."

Cole grabbed her arm; his hard eyes drilled her.

He wasn't bluffing and they both knew it. "It's now or never."

Rebecca looked at Mrs. Applegate, desperate for an ally. "I can't do this."

Mrs. Applegate smiled. "Dear, it is the best solution for everyone. Think of the boys."

"We don't love each other."

"Some of the best marriages don't start off as a love match," the older woman reasoned.

"Real love grows with time," Mr. Applegate added.

Cole cursed. "Yes or no, Rebecca. I want an answer now."

The weight of her decision pressed against her chest. She glanced at Mac and Dusty who stared expectantly at her. Mrs. Applegate held her breath, while Mr. Applegate gripped the brim of his hat.

"Yes or no," Cole persisted.

"*I* hate you," she whispered.

His lips curled into a smug smile. He'd won and they both knew it.

"Yes or no."

"Yes."

Chapter Thirteen

Rebecca glanced at the small Swiss clock that sat on the mantel above the fireplace in her room. It read 11:44. An hour had passed since Cole had declared they'd marry and only minutes remained before the judge arrived at the inn to perform the ceremony.

It was her wedding day and she was miserable.

Rebecca stared into the tall oval mirror in the corner of her room. She'd donned a freshly laundered green muslin dress and tied back her hair with a yellow ribbon. Her pasty cheeks looked sunken and hollow, and dark rings hung under her eyes.

She turned from the mirror and sank down onto the edge of her bed. Bess had taken the children, declaring all brides needed a moment or two to themselves before the wedding. The house was quiet except for the steady thud of Cole's pacing.

Then his footsteps stopped and a silence descended over the house. Unnatural, the quiet reminded her that she'd lose her children without this marriage.

Clutching damp palms together, Rebecca rose and walked to the window. She lifted the lace curtains and looked over her front yard, where dozens of townsfolk had gathered to witness the nuptials.

The town women scurried about a buffet table they'd set under a large shade tree. The decision had been made to resume the interrupted Fourth of July activities of yesterday and turn Cole and Rebecca's wedding into a party. Mrs. Applegate had marshaled the women in record time and put together a feast any bride would be proud of.

The last time Rebecca had married, she'd eloped. There'd been no one present at the simple ceremony, and she and Curtis had spoken their vows without fanfare in the modest Denver vicarage. Still, Rebecca had been full of girlish excitement. Curtis had looked so dashing in his camel suit, lace cuffs and polished black boots. She'd had so much hope for the future.

Now, only dread filled her heart.

She knew how difficult life could be when a marriage went sour. She'd loved Curtis—or at least thought she had—and things had turned out miserably for them. So, what hope did she and Cole have when at the outset there was only distrust and bitterness?

A loud knock on the door startled Rebecca from her thoughts. "Come in."

The door creaked open and Mrs. Applegate popped her head in. "You decent?"

Rebecca rose. "Yes, I'm dressed."

"Splendid. You don't mind a few visitors before the wedding do you?"

Yes. "No."

"Good." Mrs. Applegate's ample bosom swayed as she bounded in the room, basket in hand. Prudence followed with an armful of flowers tied together with a white ribbon. "We've come to see that you're properly outfitted."

Rebecca smoothed palms over her skirt. "I am ready."

Mrs. Applegate tittered. "All brides deserve a few finishing touches that make them special. It isn't every day you get married."

Thankfully.

"Now let's have a look at that hair of yours," Prudence said.

Rebecca touched the curly strands. "What's wrong with my hair?"

"It should sit atop your head," said Prudence. "Like a queen."

"I don't feel much like a queen."

Prudence squeezed Rebecca's icy hand. "I know and I'm sorry. If I'd held my tongue yesterday, your wedding day to Cole would have been a happy one and not so filled with anger."

Rebecca's heart twisted as she stared into Prudence's watery eyes. She couldn't disguise her bitterness. "If you'd not spoken up, there'd never have been a wedding."

Mrs. Applegate snorted. "Oh, there'd have been a wedding between the two of you sooner or later. Even a blind man could have seen that one."

Rebecca glanced up, shocked. "Ridiculous."

"The man can't keep his eyes off you. Everyone could see that."

"Cole hates me."

Prudence shrugged. "He wouldn't be so mad if he didn't care."

Mrs. Applegate winked. "Wounded pride. Men are like babies when you hurt their pride."

"I didn't mean to hurt him. I was afraid to trust him."

"We know, dear," Mrs. Applegate said patting her on the shoulder. "I think it's safe to say we all misjudged Cole McGuire."

"He'll never forgive me."

"Men need to lick their wounds," Prudence soothed. "He'll forgive and forget. Give him time."

Rebecca doubted Prudence's words, but didn't have the chance to say so. Mrs. Applegate glanced at the clock. "Time! That's one thing we don't have much of. Cole was insistent that we have you downstairs at twelve noon sharp."

"Said he'd come and get you himself if you were a minute late," Prudence said.

"How romantic," Mrs. Applegate cooed as she guided Rebecca in front of her full-length mirror. "I wish my Gene showed that kind of fire for me. Honestly, I think the man gets more excited about a clean house and a hot meal these days than he does me."

Prudence giggled as she laid her bundle of flowers on the bed. "Fresh laundry made my late husband go weak at the knees."

The women laughed as they arranged Rebecca's hair. She let the banter drift above her head and wondered if there might be some hope she and Cole could one day build a happy marriage.

She thought about the dance they'd shared only yesterday—the touch of his palm pressing into her back, the way his natural scent mingled with soap, and the hard feel of his chest as it grazed against her.

He despised her bitterly, yet she craved his touch. Where was the sense of independence she'd guarded so carefully these last few years?

"Why, Rebecca, you should always wear your hair up," Mrs. Applegate declared. She stepped back, brush in hand, to survey her work. "You look lovely."

The upswept style drew attention to Rebecca's high cheekbones and creamy white skin. She tucked a stray curl behind her ear. "It's lovely."

"You're lovely," Mrs. Applegate said.

"Now for the finishing touches," Prudence declared, turning toward the bouquet of flowers and picking several from the pile.

She twisted several delicate blue flowers from their stems and pinned them into Rebecca's hair. "These are columbines that grow wild behind my house. Columbines are for gentleness. May your groom's heart be filled with gentleness."

Touched by Prudence's sentiment, Rebecca admired the dainty crown.

Mrs. Applegate retrieved the bundle of flowers from the bed. "Each of the ladies in town donated flowers from their garden so that you'd have an extra special bouquet."

Prudence fussed over a bent petal. "The roses are from my garden. They represent love and beauty."

"I picked the ivy so you'll have a long life," said Mrs. Applegate. "And Olivia Farthing picked the daises—so you'd always have sunshine in your life."

Rebecca fingered the fragile blossoms. Touched by their friendship, her heart overflowed with hope and joy. "You have all been so good to me."

Mrs. Applegate pulled a lace handkerchief from her sleeve and dried Rebecca's tears. "If you start that again, I'm liable to start blubbering like a babe."

Rebecca sniffed, trying to stem the tide of fresh tears. The clock on the wall began to chime as the second hand swept toward noon—*one, two, three...* "I'm afraid."

Four, five, six.

Prudence squeezed her hand. "You'll be fine. Just wait and see."

Seven, eight, nine.

"Are you certain he cares?" Rebecca hated the desperation that had crept into her voice.

Ten, eleven, twelve.

"Cole is a man of action, not words, and no matter how angry his words, always remember, he came back to you," Mrs. Applegate said as she gave Rebecca a final hug and opened the door. "And he didn't have to marry you."

Rebecca followed, uncertain of how she found the courage to put one foot in front of the other.

Prudence sniffed back a tear and hurried ahead of Rebecca. "I'll tell the fiddler to start playing."

From the top of the staircase, she heard the din of voices mingling on the front porch. By the sound of it, she imagined the entire town had turned out for her and Cole's wedding.

Mrs. Applegate smoothed a curl off Rebecca's forehead and sniffed back a tear. "You look beautiful, dear."

Rebecca squeezed the older woman's hand then moved toward the stairs.

Just then the front door opened with a bang. Cole appeared at the threshold. His feet were braced apart as if he were ready for a fight.

He wore a clean white shirt—the top three unfastened buttons forming a V at the base of his throat. Dark pants hugged his muscular thighs. He'd cinched a belt tightly at his narrow waist and brushed the mud from his scuffed boots.

He conjured images of a pirate not a bridegroom and for a moment, Rebecca was half tempted to flee.

Cole glared up at her. When his eyes met hers, he blinked as if he didn't quite believe what he saw. The hard lines around his eyes softened and he strode to the base of the stairs and waited for Rebecca. "We're ready for you."

Rebecca clutched her bouquet until her knuckles

ached. The top stair creaked as she took her first step. She was certain her knees would buckle if she didn't move carefully.

Cole's gaze remained riveted on her until she reached his side. He took her elbow and for an instant, he looked as if he'd speak, but instead he muttered an oath and guided her to the open front door and out onto the porch.

As she suspected, all the people in White Stone had gathered in her yard. Bess stood beside a stern-faced sheriff and the boys, Mac in his brown dress pants and white shirt and Dusty in his new denims and red shirt. Even Ernie nodded with approval. The children's faces split into wide grins when they saw her. Rebecca smiled.

Thumb in mouth, Mac said, "Mama."

Dusty nodded. "Miss Rebecca."

Rebecca knelt in front of the children, mindful that Cole stood behind her, his body rigid. "My, don't you two look fine today."

Mac touched the flowers circling Rebecca's head. "Flowers."

"Yes." Her throat tightened and only through force of will did she keep her voice even. "I love you two very much."

Dusty hugged Rebecca tight. "I love you, too."

At Cole's impatient touch, she rose, her throat tight with unshed tears. She winked at the boys, then moistening her lips, allowed Cole to guide her toward the west end of the porch.

A tall, pencil-thin man waited. He wore a gray suit, dusty cuffs and collar, a neat bowl-shaped hat and held a floppy Bible in his long bony fingers. "Good afternoon," he said in a deep, clear voice.

"Rebecca, this is Judge Bruce," Cole said smoothly.

She nodded to the judge. "Thank you for coming on such short notice." Blast her ingrained manners. Why was she thanking him?

The judge offered a wan smile and pulled a pair of wire-rim glasses from his pocket. "My stage leaves in fifteen minutes, so let's get on with this."

"We're ready," Cole said in a clear, even voice.

I'm not! The words danced on the tip of Rebecca's tongue.

Cole took his place at her side. The top of Rebecca's head barely reached his shoulder. She marveled at his height and strength and prayed Mrs. Applegate's assessment of him was true.

Always remember, he came back to you.

The judge cleared his throat. "Dearly, beloved, we are gathered here today to join together this man and woman in matrimony. Do you, Cole McGuire, take this woman to be your lawful wife?"

"I do," he said without hesitation.

"Do you, uh—" the judged paused and checked his scribbled notes on the back of a tattered envelope "—Rebecca Elizabeth Sinclair Taylor take Cole McGuire to be your husband?"

Before she could answer, Mac broke away from Bess, ran to Rebecca and hugged her legs. "My mama."

Rebecca patted Mac on his back. "Honey, I'm not going anywhere."

"He's taking you."

"No, he's not."

A tide of low whispers swept over the crowd. Rebecca knelt down and chucked her child under the chin. "Honey, I'm not going anywhere."

Cole knelt down in front of the child, all traces of tension gone. He smoothed a long finger over the child's pudgy cheek. "Your ma's right. She's not leaving. I'm moving in here to live with you, Dusty and your ma for good."

"Why?"

"Because your ma and I are getting married."

"Why?"

The muscle in the side of his jaw twitched as he hesitated. "It's the right thing to do. From now on we'll be a family."

Dusty frowned. "Me, too, Cole?"

"You, too," he said patting his shoulder. "From now on I'll be your pa as well as Mac's."

Rebecca's throat stung with emotion. "Do you mean that?" she whispered.

He rose and met her gaze. "I'll do right by both of them."

"Thank you."

Cole hoisted Mac up. The boy settled easily in his arms, happy for the extra attention. "I believe you owe the judge an answer."

Rebecca stared into Cole's direct gaze, searching for any sign that his heart held the tiniest bit of affection for her. She saw anger, fury and yes, passion. The latter gave her a measure of hope. Perhaps the barrier between love and hate were closer than she thought. "Yes, I'll marry him."

The judge expelled the breath he was holding. "By the powers vested in me by the state of Colorado, I pronounce you man and wife. You may now kiss the bride."

She and Cole were married.

The thought left Rebecca strangely exhilarated.

Clearly Cole loved the children as much as she did. Together they would find a way past the anger and hurt and forge a friendship. Theirs might not be a love match now, but given time anything was possible.

As Mrs. Applegate had said, Cole was a man of action and few words. Rebecca knew words meant nothing to Cole. She would have to *show* him she was sorry for her lie. She'd make him the best wife he could hope for.

Rebecca turned to leave, doubting Cole would want to kiss her in front of all these people. Likely, he was still brimming with anger and she didn't want to test his patience.

But as Rebecca moved toward the well-wishers, Cole handed Mac to Bess and banded his long fingers around her narrow wrist. The lean planes of his face didn't soften a fraction. "You owe me a kiss."

"B-but...' she stammered, her gaze darting among the smiling faces.

Cole gathered her in his arms, not giving her another chance to speak. The quick beat of his heart pounded under her palm.

He kissed her and to her surprise, she didn't care that the entire town surrounded them. He tightened his hold and in one searing moment deepened their kiss. Dark, erotic sensations flickered to life deep in her bones.

She leaned into him, limp and wanting, savoring the way his rough skin made her skin tingle.

Gene Applegate cleared his throat. "Now, there's time enough for that."

Prudence and Mrs. Applegate snickered.

Cole broke the kiss and stepped back, a frown

marring his face. Rebecca stood in stunned silence, staring at him and shaken to the core.

Mrs. Applegate tapped her on the shoulder. "Dear, is everything all right?"

Rebecca touched her fingertips to her lips then looked around at the dozens of onlookers who stared boldly at them, many with their mouths agape. Color burned her cheeks. "Yes, of course."

"Good, then let's have the band strike up a tune in honor of Mr. and Mrs. Cole McGuire."

Everyone clapped then. The women swarmed around Rebecca, giggling and joking about the kiss and wedding night. And the men circled Cole, sweeping him away as they shared a bawdy joke or two and talked of the prosperity sure to grace White Stone when the mine reopened.

It all seemed to swirl around Rebecca like a dream. Over the crowd of laughing people, she caught a glimpse of Cole. He stood tall, a good head above everyone. Longing surged in her.

As if sensing her appraisal, he looked up, his jaw tight. Their gazes locked. And she knew in that instant, his thoughts mirrored her own.

She *had* done the right thing by marrying him. She repeated the words over and over again even as her thoughts drifted to their wedding night. Her mouth went as dry as cotton.

Curtis had always been disappointed with her in bed, calling her clumsy, childish. She didn't want Cole to be disappointed by her lack of experience. She had to find Bess.

Chapter Fourteen

The wedding celebration was more than Rebecca could ever have expected. Mrs. Applegate and her crew of women had outdone themselves, organizing the lavish display of fruit pies, roasted chickens and breads. The entire town gathered on the picnic grounds near the church. Rebecca and Cole spent most of the afternoon standing side by side accepting the good wishes of their neighbors.

Cole's smile was quick and full, but Rebecca saw the way he clenched his jaw when no one was looking. She knew he itched to leave the festivities behind.

But there'd been no sign of Bess, and Rebecca grew more desperate with each passing minute.

As Cole reached out to shake hands with another person, his arm grazed hers. Lightning bolts shot through her body, setting all her senses on edge.

Her mouth grew dry. It had been years since she'd been held and her body ached to be loved and touched.

Seth Osborne climbed up in the bed of an empty wagon and raised a Mason jar full of whiskey. "Okay folks, gather around so that I can toast the bride and groom."

Cole, silent and stone-faced, led Rebecca toward Seth. "After this, we're leaving," he said in a gruff voice, loud enough for only her to hear.

His words fueled her worries. She found it difficult to concentrate on anything other than the palm of his hand searing through her dress into the small of her back.

Seth waited until the crowd circled around and quieted. "I reckon since I've lived in this town longer than anybody, it's my job to offer the wedding toast. I've known Cole since he was fourteen years old. I've watched Rebecca grow from a girl into a woman and been proud at the way she's mothered Mac and now Dusty." He raised his glass. "Rebecca and Cole, you're good people, and I wish you a long and happy marriage."

Rebecca's chest tightened with unspoken emotion. "Thank you."

"Thank you, Seth." Cole faced the crowd and said in a booming voice, "This has been a fine celebration, but it's time my family and I went home. Good day to you all."

"Aren't you going to stay longer? We've got sack races planned and the pie-eating contest," Mrs. Applegate said, frowning.

Rebecca, not ready to be alone with Cole, was quick to say, "Of course, we will." She pulled her arm free and hurried into the center of the crowd, allowing them to engulf her. She didn't dare look at Cole, sure that he was frowning. She presented her best smile and let the town ladies guide her over to the display of fried pies, cookies and sweet butters.

Rebecca picked up a slice of gingerbread and nibbled the end, not really tasting the confection. "This is delicious," she said, her voice a bit too enthusiastic.

Mrs. Applegate picked up two cinnamon cookies. "Prudence was beside herself yesterday when no one got a chance to eat her blue ribbon gingerbread. It'll do her heart glad to know the bride enjoyed some today."

Rebecca bit into the over-spiced confection. "It's wonderful," she lied.

"You made a pretty bride, Mrs. McGuire," Mrs. Applegate said. She dabbed a lace handkerchief to the corner of her eye.

Rebecca lowered the cookie from her lips. "*Mrs. McGuire.* That sounds so strange."

"You'll get used to it."

"Yes," she said absently.

Mrs. Applegate popped it in her mouth. "I know Cole's rough around the edges, but he does clean up mighty well."

"Yes."

Mrs. Applegate bit into a second cookie. "He helped my nephew Stan with the fire and just a half hour ago offered him a job working in the mine as foreman."

Rebecca blinked. "He did?"

"Yes, he did," she said dusting cookie crumbs from her ample bosom.

"I'm happy for you."

"You should be happy for yourself and everyone else in this town. I know Stan and Cole have had their differences, but they both want this town to grow and thrive together. They'll get that mine up and running."

"Yes, I'm sure they will," she said honestly. She doubted there was anything Cole couldn't accomplish if he set his mind to it.

Mrs. Applegate reached for a third cookie. "You look pale as a ghost."

Rebecca set the uneaten gingerbread down on the table. "I'm just tired. Have you seen Bess?"

"Not lately. Saw her talking with the sheriff an hour or so ago."

"Oh."

"I know what you're worried about," the older woman said in a hushed voice.

"Really?"

"The marriage night."

"I've been married before," she said feigning an indifference she didn't quite feel. She'd have preferred to talk to Bess about such intimate matters, but her friend was nowhere to be found. She wondered if she could solicit advice from Mrs. Applegate.

"I've often wondered what the big fuss is all about."

"That's because you married that pompous Curtis. Tonight, you'll be sleeping with a real man."

Rebecca felt the color rising in her cheeks. There was something about Cole that was larger than life, frightening almost. He stood among a group of men, holding Mac in one arm and Dusty at his side. He stood tall and straight, his gaze sure and direct.

The persistent yearning that always pestered her when he was around, returned. She studied his long, lean hands, imagining them on her naked body. She thought about lying under his muscular form, the sweat of their two bodies mingling.

Her mouth went bone dry. Mrs. Applegate was right. One way or another, after she and Cole made love, she knew she'd never be the same. Her insides turned to jelly and her knees wobbled. Tonight wasn't going to be anything like her first wedding night.

"Mrs. Applegate, about tonight. I mean, I want it to be special."

"It will, dear."

"How can I be sure?"

The old woman met her with knowing eyes. "Give in to your heart. Instinct will guide you."

"I was never sure what to do with Curtis."

"Cole will be different."

She imagined his hands threading through her hair. Her insides quivered and her knees nearly buckled.

Mrs. Applegate had told her to follow her instincts. Well, right now, instinct told her to run.

Cole hadn't been able to take his eyes off Rebecca since the moment she'd stepped out onto the landing at the top of the stairs—a vision with the ring of flowers nestled in her hair, her lips parted and full and her blue eyes wide. A fairy princess.

Five hours ago when he'd demanded this marriage, he'd not thought past protecting his rights as a father. Now that his fury had cooled, all he could see was Rebecca.

He couldn't take his eyes off her and the way her dress clung to her narrow waist and her full breasts.

Mac squirmed in Cole's arms. The child stretched his hands out to Rebecca and strained his body toward her. Cole had to hold on with both hands so the child didn't flip out of his arms.

"Mama!"

Rebecca's smile brightened. She closed the distance between them and she accepted the boy, easily, naturally. She kissed him on the cheek, tucked him on her hip, before rustling Dusty's hair with her hand. "You look mighty fine today."

"Thank you, Miss Rebecca," Dusty said.

"Wait until the girls in the schoolhouse get a look at you. They'll all be begging you to carry their books home."

Splotches of red colored his cheeks. "Ah, quit it."

"We best get home," Cole said, his voice hoarse.

Panic pinched the corners of her mouth. "So soon?"

"We've been here six hours."

"Really, that long. I didn't notice."

A twinge of guilt fueled his sour mood but the

time had come for them to go home. He didn't like seeing fear in her eyes. He took her by the elbow and started toward the Shady Grove with the boys in tow. The town cheered them on, hooting and hollering, following them down the street as if no one in White Stone had ever gotten married before.

Cole's gaze focused on the sway of her hips as she climbed the inn's front steps. He liked the way she looked a lot.

He scowled. She was a liar, he reminded himself. Couldn't be trusted.

Tersely, he leaned past her as she reached for the front door, opening it and waiting for her to enter. Doe eyes fluttered up to his, full of surprise at the unexpected courtesy.

Good. Stay off guard, Rebecca, then I can sort out my own emotions.

She brushed past him, the scent of lilacs trailing into the foyer. Dusty stumbled past while Mac, now home and on familiar ground, squirmed to get down.

Rebecca set the child down. "You boys want a snack?"

"The boys have eaten their fill today," Cole said, his tone brooking no argument. "Dusty and Mac, it's getting late and time for bed."

"Ah, come on," Dusty grumbled. He yawned.

"You need your sleep and so does Mac," Cole said.

Dusty tossed the bangs off his eyes. "Yeah, well, two weeks ago, I did as I pleased, stayed up as late as I wanted." He was testing, but there was no real punch to his words.

"Do you really want to go back to that?" Cole demanded.

"I reckon not."

Cole laid his hand on Dusty's shoulder. "Your pa's gone now, Dusty, and like it or not, we're your family now."

Dusty rubbed his eyes. "Okay, but do I have to go to bed?"

"Yes."

"Rats."

Cole smiled. Dusty was a good kid and he'd grow into a fine man one day. He felt lucky to have the boy in his life. "Let's get upstairs."

Rebecca and Cole escorted the boys upstairs. Obviously accustomed to taking care of Mac and Dusty herself, she frowned with surprise when he reached for Mac's nightshirt at the same time she did. Their fingers touched.

She blushed and moistened her lips. "I'll get the boys ready for bed."

He cleared his throat, trying to maintain control

of his body. "I said I'd be here to tuck them into bed each night and I will."

"You don't have to do this."

"I want to."

Rebecca released the nightshirt. She stood by as Dusty changed into his nightclothes and Cole deftly stripped Mac. He grimaced when it came time to change Mac's diaper.

Rebecca seemed to sense his indecision. She smiled smugly, shooed him out of the way and quickly changed Mac's wet diaper. She must have changed the boy's diapers thousands of times in the last two years and her parenting expertise emphasized his own inexperience.

Damn, he'd missed so much of Mac's life.

Minutes later, Cole leaned against the doorjamb, watching Rebecca as she kissed each boy on the forehead and drew the covers up to their chins.

A knot wrenched in his gut as he stared at her. She looked like a sprite, the soft halo of ringlets framing her face and the ring of blue flowers atop her head. There was a faint blush to her cheeks.

"Perhaps, the boys would like a bedtime story?"

"Tomorrow."

"But it settles them down."

"They'll sleep like the dead tonight."

"Of course."

She was White Stone's very own princess, a beauty coveted by all men who laid eyes on her.

And it struck him then that this fragile woman had the power to crush his heart.

Rebecca's heart skipped a beat when she saw Cole leaning against the doorjamb, his hands tucked under his arms. The naked longing in his eyes took her breath away. She summoned all her will just to put one foot in front of the other and walk to him. She wanted this night to be perfect.

Let instinct guide you.

''They're exhausted,'' she whispered.

He nodded, not saying a word as he took her by the hand. His hand was rough and his grip firm as he led her toward her room. She didn't resist.

Cole tugged her into the bedroom and closed the door behind them with a soft click. She licked her dry lips as he turned and moved toward her, as silent as a cougar.

He cupped her face in his hands. ''You are beautiful.'' His voice was a hoarse whisper.

Color burned her cheeks. ''Thank you.''

He touched the circle of flowers in her hair then drew his callused fingertips down the side of her cheek, sending a thousand shivers dancing down her spine. Cupping her face in his hands, he pressed his lips to hers and devoured her. He tasted of salt and a hint of whiskey.

Rebecca's body screamed with a lifetime of unsatisfied longings. She never tasted the sweet anticipation other women whispered about until now.

Instinct. Instinct. Instinct.

She stood on tiptoe and wrapped her arms around Cole's neck and pressed her breasts against his chest. Her nipples hardened into soft peaks and strained against the fabric of her bodice. Liquid heat seared her body.

A growl rumbled from Cole's chest before he scooped her up in his arms and carried her to the bed.

The room was dark, except for the red-orange glow of the setting sun streaming through the window. Shadows sharpened the hard lines of Cole's face, now rigid with desire. He laid her in the center of the soft mattress. The springs creaked when he straddled her. He cupped her breasts with his hands and teased the nipples with his thumbs.

The blood pounding in Rebecca's body fueled her wanting. She arched toward Cole and slid her hands up his muscular thighs, sending him a silent invitation—an olive branch.

He snaked his fingers through her hair, pulling it free of the pins until it cascaded in a waterfall of curls around her head on the white pillow.

He unfastened the buttons of her bodice, one by one, until he reached her waist. He pushed back the folds of her bodice and stared at the creamy white tops of her breasts cresting over her corset and chemise.

"You're so beautiful." He lowered his lips to the soft mounds and kissed the hollow between them. His unshaved chin rubbed against her soft skin, sending shivers of delight through her body. She cupped the back of his head, threading her fingers through his coarse black hair.

Deftly, Cole untied the pink buttons of her chemise then unfastened the hooks of her corset. Her breasts, full and ripe, spilled out for him. He leaned over her, his gaze dark and intent, and suckled her nipples. He took his time tasting her.

Rebecca groaned, arching into him. Desire speared into her womb, making coherent thought impossible.

Cole released one breast and trailed his hand under her skirt, up the inside of her leg. He yanked at the drawstring of her pantaloons. A soft ripping sound rent the air. And then he was touching that most private part of her that pulsed for his touch.

Cole's long fingers touched her moist flesh, rubbing the nub until she moaned his name over and over again. Her senses teetered close to the edge of a mysterious abyss when he suddenly stopped.

Her eyes flew open. All manner of pride gone, she pleaded for him to continue. He climbed off the bed, but his gaze still pierced her.

Without speaking a word, he quickly pulled off his boots, shirt and finally his pants. He stood before her for one maddening heartbeat, his manhood proud and erect.

Instinct. Instinct.

She didn't want to run this time. Her only thoughts were of him inside her, satisfying her growing drumbeat of desire.

Cole climbed on top of her, then he pushed her skirts up to her waist, and pulled her pantaloons down over the tops of her high-buttoned black boots.

A hint of a smile touched Cole's lips. He needed no further coaxing. He straddled her, pressed his manhood against her tender flesh, then drove into her.

She felt the harlot, making love to him half-dressed, but she didn't care. She wanted him. Shameless as a fallen dove, she spread her legs for him, inviting him in.

She sucked in a breath through her clenched teeth. Her taut body stretched to accommodate him. He groaned his pleasure as he paused, seemingly savoring the feel of her tight hold on him.

Then he began to move in the ancient rhythm,

plunging back and forth inside her. She matched his movements, tilting her pelvis to meet his thrusts.

Sweat beaded on his forehead as he stared down at her.

He bent his head and suckled her breasts as he moved inside her. She whimpered his name over and over again, praying he would release her from this sweet agony.

Finally, after many maddening minutes—or hours—he lowered his hand to her tender flesh and began to rub as he moved inside her.

Her senses exploded like a burst of lightning. She arched her back and sucked her breath in between her clenched teeth.

Cole drove into her with all his strength, filling her and taking her over the edge into sweet oblivion.

He groaned her name as he clenched the sheets on either side of her head. She felt his muscles tighten and constrict before he collapsed against her, his body glistening with a sheen of sweat.

His heart hammered against her naked breast, matching her own racing beat. Minutes ticked by as they lay together as one.

Basking in the warmth of his body, she never felt more complete or alive. Hope filled her. She stroked a dark curl on his chest, wrapping it around her finger. Unlike Curtis, she liked touching Cole.

As she slid her hand over the flat of his belly he tensed. Unsure, she stopped and looked at him. Desire no longer clouded his eyes. His expression had turned hard, unreadable.

"Cole."

Silent, he pushed himself off her and swung his legs over the side of the bed. She touched his naked back. He flinched and moved away from her. He reached for his pants and put them on.

She rolled on her side, confused, still dazed from desire. She tugged the comforter over her naked breasts, suddenly feeling vulnerable. "Where are you going?"

"To my room."

Confusion clouded her thoughts. "Why? I thought after what just happened, everything was going to be different between us. Didn't I please you?"

"Yes." The word sounded as if it were ripped from his chest.

"Then stay the night with me."

He reached for his boots and shirt. His gaze bore into her. "No."

A sharp pain stabbed her insides. "But we just made love. You said I pleased you."

"A marriage isn't just about physical pleasure,

Rebecca. There has to be trust as well. And I don't trust you.''

Her throat constricted. ''But in time, you will learn to trust me.''

He stood over the bed, glaring at her. ''I need to go.''

She felt dirty, used. ''I thought things had changed between us.''

Cole turned and stalked out of the room, leaving her cold, devastated and alone with her tears.

Chapter Fifteen

Two weeks had passed since their wedding night and the sound of Rebecca's sobs still echoed in Cole's mind.

When they'd made love, she'd touched the deepest part of his soul. He'd felt utterly defenseless and it had scared the hell out of him. The unwelcome vulnerability coupled with his raw anger had driven him to lash out blindly at her.

Now that he'd had time to cool off, he regretted like hell that he'd acted so harshly to her. But he'd been unable to breach the growing divide between them.

A knock on his mine office door shattered the silence. Cole glanced up from the stack of papers arranged on a makeshift desk of wood and sawhorses. Little more than a shack, the small structure served as his base of operations. A cold potbellied stove stood in the corner and only one grimy window offered a view of the mine entrance. A lantern on the corner of his desk flickered, supplementing the morning sun's faint glow.

"Come in," he growled.

Wade shoved open the door and marched in. His cheeks glowed and his eyes sparkled. "Well, you sound as prickly as a bear."

"I am."

Wade closed the door behind him. "If I had such a pretty little wife at home like you, I'd hate having to come into work too."

"Right."

Wade had accepted Cole and Rebecca's marriage without trouble. In truth, the older man had almost seemed relieved.

As far as everyone in town was concerned, Cole and Rebecca's marriage was the perfect match.

Cole and Rebecca shared a polite and civilized marriage when they were in public. She laughed easily around the children, showering each with affection. They attended Sunday services together and they'd both walked Dusty to school on his first day.

But when they were alone Rebecca became quiet and distant. She kept a plate warm for him each evening, but while he ate in the dim lantern light, she'd bid him good evening, climb the stairs and retreat to her room alone.

They looked like a family, but in truth were not.

"What can I do for you?" Cole said rising.

The sheriff strode over to the desk and set a basket down on it. "Bess sent me. She figured if Mohammed wouldn't come to the mountain, then the mountain..." he said, letting his voice trail. "She thought you might like lunch."

Cole forced his shoulders to relax and lifted the red-checked napkin. Inside he found fried chicken, biscuits and two slices of pie. "Thanks."

"She wants to know if you're coming home for dinner."

"Since when did you become Bess's messenger?"

Wade shrugged. "I reckon I like helping her when I can."

"She's sweet on you."

Wade grinned. "Yeah, I know."

"You told her that?" Cole liked Bess and he didn't want to see her hurt.

"I reckon I will sooner or later."

"Make it sooner."

Wade shoved his hands in his pockets glancing at the stack of papers on Cole's desk. "Things moving along well here?"

"Just fine."

"Everyone's wondering when you'll hit a new vein."

"Hard to say."

The day after the wedding the town council had agreed to waive all back taxes on the Lucky Star if Rebecca willingly turned over operations to Cole. As her husband, he could have seized control without her permission, but the council's tax waiver depended on her cooperation. He'd expected her to resist, but without a fuss, Rebecca had signed the papers giving him total control of the Lucky Star.

The substantial savings had been a real boon to the mine, giving him the extra resources to hire additional workers. He was already a month ahead of schedule.

"Folks is also wondering if you've forgiven Rebecca for fibbing to you?"

Cole frowned. "Fibbing. She tried to keep my son from me."

"She's real sorry."

Cole thrust out a sigh. "Wade, what the devil are you doing here?"

He picked up a piece of paper off Cole's desk and pretended to study it. "Just a friendly visit."

Cole snatched the paper away. "Did Rebecca send you here?"

Wade chuckled. "If she knew I'd come to see

you, she'd skin me alive. Naw, Bess sent me. Figured we should talk man to man."

"About what?"

Wade scratched his chin. "Your marriage. Bess wants to be certain things are going well between you and your wife."

"Tell Bess to talk to Rebecca."

"She has, but it seems Rebecca's been real tight-lipped."

Pride nudged him. His wife was no gossip. She kept her own counsel. "Don't worry about Rebecca and me. We'll survive."

He snorted. "That mean you've forgiven her?"

Cole raked his fingers through his hair. "I understand now why she lied about Mac."

Wade's eyes brightened. "That so?"

"I understand that as a woman alone, she was desperate and weak."

Wade bristled. "Rebecca's one of the strongest people I know." He cracked his knuckles and turned toward the window. "You know I had a child once?"

"No, I didn't."

"It was a long time ago." His eyes grew vacant as if he'd returned to a time long ago. "Davie was a towheaded little fellow just like your Mac."

Cole stood silent, unsure of what to say.

"Lost my son and wife to cholera back in '61.

I reckon what attracted me to Rebecca was she came with a ready-made family." His eyes filled with tears. "Damn, what I would give to have my wife and son back."

Cole's anger drained from him. He stared at the sheriff's slumped shoulders. He seemed to grow old before his eyes.

Wade sniffed. "So I reckon I know what it feels like to have a child and lose one."

"I'm sorry."

Wade pierced Cole with his gaze. "I'd do anything to get my boy back even if it meant lying, cheating, stealing or worse."

Cole clenched his fingers. "What would you have done if someone tried to keep him from you?"

Wade cocked an eyebrow. "Can't say. But I do know it ain't right to blame Rebecca for trying to do what she thought was best for her child."

A heavy silence fell between them. Cole knew Rebecca loved Mac—it was one of the things he'd grown to admire about her. "I wanted her to trust me."

"Her son's future was on the line and she didn't know you from Adam. And let's face it, you didn't have a squeaky clean reputation when you lived in town."

Cole couldn't deny Wade's logic.

Wade grunted. "Eat your vittles before they get cold. I got to get cleaned up so I can take Bess for a ride in the country."

Before Cole could respond, the old man strode out the door past Stan Farthing who stood with his hand raised, poised to knock. Cold air rushed into the stuffy cabin.

Stan cleared his throat. "The dozen men you hired are outside waiting for orders."

"Good." Cole rose, grabbed his hat.

Cole and Stan had struggled through an awkward few days, but had settled into a businesslike arrangement that suited them both. Stan's supply connections in Denver coupled with Cole's bankroll and management skills had complemented each other.

Everything was going well and if his fortune held, the Lucky Star would soon be releasing silver.

If only he could manage his marriage as smoothly.

Stan hesitated. He rubbed his hand over his freshly shaved chin. "The fate of White Stone rests on your shoulders now."

"On all our shoulders."

"Folks are hoping for the best, but I don't think most believe you'll find silver."

Cole squinted as he stared into the sun. "When

the odds are against me, I'm at my best. I'm a gambler at heart.''

"You really believe there's silver in there?''

"Yep.''

"Think it'll be easy to reach?''

"Nope, the free silver is gone. We're gonna have to work for everything we find now.''

"I'm willing to work, as long as it brings prosperity back to White Stone.'' Stan shoved a dirty hand through his hair. "Look, I'm sorry for the things I said when you first came to town.''

"Forget it.''

"I can't. My family would have gone hungry without you. Hell, after the fight we had years ago, I couldn't blame you if you turned your back on me.''

"What's past is past, Stan.'' He held out his hand.

Standing stock straight, he accepted Cole's hand and shook it. "I'm glad to be on your crew.''

"Good.''

"Well, let me get to work.'' He headed toward the mine entrance then he stopped. "Oh, I thought it best you know—Dusty's pa came back in town late last night. I saw him at the Rosebud.''

Every muscle in Cole's body stiffened. "What's he want?''

"Dusty, I reckon.''

* * *

"Papa!" Mac shouted. He ran into the kitchen, carrying a toy truck Cole had carved for him. "Papa's home!"

Rebecca looked up from the sink. "Papa? You mean Cole?" The child had started calling Cole Papa days ago, but it still sounded strange to Rebecca's ears.

"Yes, Papa!"

Mac had forged a strong bond with Cole, as if he had craved a man's attention all his life. She was glad Mac was growing to love his father.

Drying her hands on a kitchen towel, Rebecca followed Mac toward the front door. Nervous excitement mingled with dread.

Cole never came home in the middle of the day so likely Mac had spotted a traveler in need of a room. Cole had insisted that there'd be no more boarders at the inn, but that hadn't stopped the stray person from stopping. She'd sent them all to the Rosebud.

"Honey, Papa is at the mine."

These last two weeks had been the loneliest of her life. Cole spent most of his waking hours with the boys or at the mine and he barely had spoken to her, let alone offered her any tenderness.

Mac ran out the front door, Rebecca on his heels. She stopped on the porch when she saw

Cole. Covered in dirt and grime, striding up the walkway, he still possessed grace and confidence. Her heart skipped a beat.

Cole scooped Mac up in his arms tossing him high in the air. "Hey, partner. You having a good day?"

"Truck."

The creases around Cole's eyes deepened. "So I see."

Rebecca managed a smile. "Everything all right at the mine?" It was a simple question, but with all the anger that had passed between them, she stumbled over the words.

"All's well," he said. "The central mine shaft is in better shape than we first thought and the ten men we've hired are hardworking. If our luck holds, excavation could begin next month."

"That mine was Papa's dream. I never thought I'd see that mine open again," she said quietly.

"Your father had good instincts. He knew there was more silver to be had in the Lucky Star and I intend to find it."

Cole stood proud and tall, his voice full of unspoken confidence. If anyone could make the mine work, her husband would. Unexpected pride swelled in Rebecca. "I'm glad things are going well."

He set Mac down. "We'd not be making such

good progress if you hadn't agreed to add me as a
full partner.''

It had been an olive branch. "We're a team."

"Yes."

"What are you doing home so early in the
day?''

His gaze roamed the front lawn. "Just needed a
break. Where's Dusty?''

"He and Jared are fishing."

"He knows to stay clear of barns and lit ci-
gars?''

Rebecca smiled. "I don't think Dusty will ever
touch a cigar again.''

"When's he due back?''

"An hour or so.''

Cole drew in a deep breath. "I don't like the
idea of him running around like an urchin. I'd
rather he stay close to home.''

"Dusty's got a good head on his shoulders and
he knows White Stone just about as well as anyone. He'll be fine.''

"Still, I'd rather he stay close to home.''

She frowned. "Is there a problem?''

"No. But I'd rather he help you out around here
instead of running around the countryside.''

"He's done all his chores.''

His lips drew into a tight line as if the answer
didn't satisfy him.

"What's wrong?"

Before Cole could respond, Dusty strolled up the front walk, his pants rolled up to his knees, a fishing pole over one shoulder and a pail in the other.

Dusty's face brightened at the sight of Cole. "What are you doing home so early?"

Cole's shoulders relaxed a fraction. "Catch any fish?"

Mac ran to Dusty and pointed inside the pail. "Fish! Fish!"

Cole peered in the rusted pail and saw two six-inch fish lying wide-eyed in the bottom.

Mac picked up one of the fish only to have it slide out of his hands. "Yuck."

Dusty rolled his eyes. "I think they'll taste great for dinner."

"I couldn't agree more," Rebecca said. "Fresh fish is always a treat."

Cole examined the fish. "Where'd you catch them?"

"I've got a secret fishing spot. No one knows about it."

Rebecca smiled. "Is it the one under the willow tree next to Miller's Pond?"

Dusty's jaw dropped. "Hey, how'd you know about my secret spot?"

"You spent most of the late spring up by that pond."

"How'd you know that?"

Rebecca folded her arms over her chest. "I know more about you than you realize."

Cole cocked an eyebrow, curious. "I thought you just met the boy a few weeks ago."

"I may have just met him, but I've known about him for a long time."

"What do you know about me?"

"I know you like cherry pie better than apple. You always sat behind the saloon right after Seth swept it out, and went through the dust looking for coins."

"Hey! I thought no one saw me."

She smiled. "Dusty Saunders, do you really think I didn't know you were taking all those pies from my windowsill?"

Dusty shrugged. "I figured you just weren't paying attention."

"I saw you steal the very first pie back in April and I watched you sit out under the oak tree and eat it. You didn't think I could see, but I could."

"Why didn't you come after me?"

"Because I could see you were hungry."

He scrunched up his brow. "What about the blanket and pillow that I found in the hayloft?"

"I didn't want you getting cold at night."

"Dang," Dusty said shaking his head. "And I thought I was pulling one over on you."

"Oh, but you were a careful one. I had to hide real well otherwise you stayed clear of the house."

Cole patted the boy on the back. "Better men than you have been fooled by a woman."

The comment was made spontaneously, not intended to hold hidden meaning, but Rebecca flinched. She folded her arms over her chest again.

Cole, sensing the shift in her mood, cleared his throat. "Dusty, do me a favor and take Mac in the house. Rebecca and I need to talk over a few things."

"Sure, Cole. Come on, Mac. I smelled cookies baking this morning."

"Don't get too carried away," Rebecca warned. "Dinner's in two hours."

"We'll stop at five cookies," Dusty said, grinning.

"Stop at two," Rebecca amended.

Rebecca and Cole watched Mac scamper behind Dusty into the house. She was proud of her boys, truly grateful to have them.

"Why'd you look after Dusty?" Cole asked. "No one else in this town did."

"No child should go hungry or be mistreated."

He studied her as if he sensed there was more to her caring for the boy. "And...?"

"And when I saw him running around town, half-starved with bad shoes and no one to care for him, I saw Mac. After Lily died, no one wanted him or cared what happened to him, either.''

Cole clenched his fists and his expression darkened. Rebecca had saved Mac from God knows what kind of life and for that he'd always be in her debt.

A tense silence fell between them before he finally said, ''What do you know about Judd Saunders?''

The unexpected turn in the conversation surprised her but she kept it to herself. ''He doesn't come to town often, but I've seen enough of him to know he's a dirty, mean drunk. The first time I saw the two of them in town, Judd was smacking Dusty around, demanding the boy find work.''

Cole's fingers balled into fists. ''Shame I wasn't there.''

''I wish you had been.''

''Did he just up and leave the boy?''

''His wife died in the spring. Once she was gone, there was no one to protect the boy from Judd. I suppose it's a blessing he abandoned Dusty in town.''

Cole seemed to absorb the information. ''I see.''

''Why are you asking so many questions about Judd?''

He shrugged. ''Curious.'' He glanced up at the house. ''Do me a favor, keep Dusty close to home.

I don't like him running wild. He may think he knows how to take care of himself, but he doesn't.''

"Cole, the boy has got a level head.''

"Please make sure Dusty stays close to home unless you're with him.''

His tone rankled her nerves. "I've been a parent longer than you and I think I know what's best for Dusty.''

Fury blazed in Cole's eyes. He was a man accustomed to having his orders followed. "I expect you to do as I say.''

She sucked in a deep breath, trying to keep her voice even. "Give me a reason to.''

"You don't need a reason when I give an order.''

"This isn't the army, Cole, and I'm not one of your soldiers.''

His jaw tensed. "Don't push me, Rebecca.''

Rebecca's temper snapped. "I'll do what I think is best!'' With that, she turned on her heel and slammed the front door behind her.

Standing in the foyer, she wrapped her shaking arms around her chest. How had her life become such a miserable mess?

Before she could entertain the first answer, the front door slammed open. Cole stood in the doorway, his body rigid with fury.

Chapter Sixteen

How dare she walk away from him!

Cole felt as if the demons of hell nipped at his feet as he stood in the doorway staring at Rebecca. She had the power to stir his passions and anger like no other woman and he was certain she was driving him mad. "I'm not finished with you."

Rebecca smothered her shock with renewed anger. "I don't want to talk to you."

Before he could fire off another order, she turned on her heel and marched up the stairs.

He yanked off his hat and threw it on a chair. "Where the hell are you going?"

"Away from you!"

He marched after her and would have snatched her off the stairs if Bess hadn't stepped out of the parlor and blocked his path. A dust rag in one hand, she glowered at him as a mother hen would protecting her young. "And just where do you think you're going?"

"To talk to my wife," he ground out. He watched Rebecca scurry up the stairs. He heard her door slam closed.

"Not until that temper of yours cools." She planted her feet, ready to do battle.

Cole could have brushed past her with little effort, but he didn't. He sucked in a deep breath through clenched teeth. "Bess, this is between Rebecca and me."

"The way you were shouting, I'd say half the town's heard what you've had to say."

He stabbed fingers through his hair. "It's not my fault she's so damn hardheaded."

"The pot calls the kettle black."

"I'm not hardheaded. I'm logical and reasonable and she's a fool if she can't see that. I'm only doing what's best for her."

Her face creased with a frown. "Spoken like a true man."

He thrust out a sigh. "I need to talk to Rebecca."

"You've waited this long, you can wait another minute." She motioned toward the library and started to walk toward it, fully expecting him to follow.

He did.

The room was just as it always was—stuffed with books and oversize chairs. Sunlight trickled into the room through lace curtains, giving the room a warm, inviting look.

Bess tucked her dust rag in her apron. "What's eating at you?"

"Oh, I don't know," he said, sarcasm lacing his words. "I've got more work than three men could do in a lifetime and a wife who's acting like a spoiled child."

"I'd say you both are doing a fair imitation of that."

"Make your point, Bess."

"You're not the kind of man to come home in the middle of the day unless you're half dead with illness or something is terribly wrong."

"Nothing's wrong."

"Liar."

A mixture of wisdom and cunning sparked in her eyes. There wasn't any point in lying to her. She'd find out the truth soon enough. "Judd Saunders is back in town."

Her eyes narrowed. "What's that snake doing in town?"

Cole shook his head, a bitter smile curling his lips. "Stan saw him at the Rosebud last night. He says he's here for Dusty."

She rubbed her chin, losing herself to thought.

"Judd's got a real problem with the bottle. Likely it'll take a day or two before he sobers up. But Stan's right, when he's dried up he'll come a looking for his boy. He always does."

"He gave up all rights to that boy when he abandoned him."

Bess shook her head. "Likely he don't see it that way. The boy is his son."

Cole sank into a chair, letting his long arms flop over the sides. "What the hell do I do?"

"Only one thing you can do. Talk to him. See if you can work out an arrangement so he'll let Dusty stay."

He pictured Dusty sauntering up the front walk with the fishing pole on his shoulder. He couldn't bear the thought of him hungry or covered in bruises. "What if he takes him away?"

"You sound like Rebecca."

Cole pinned Bess with his gaze. "Our situations are completely different."

"That so?"

"I'm nothing like Judd."

"Rebecca didn't know that when you first rode into town looking rougher than a prairie dog that got tangled with a cougar."

"I'd been on the trail for two months. I didn't worry about my appearance. I was coming to get my boy."

''She didn't know what you'd do, just like you don't know what Judd is gonna do.''

Cole shot to his feet. ''I know what Judd's going to do. And I sure as hell am not going to let him lay a hand on Dusty.''

''You told any of this to Rebecca?''

''No!''

''Why not?''

Frustrated, he paced back and forth. ''She doesn't need to worry over something I can take care of.''

''She's loves Dusty just as much as you. You need to trust her with your worries.''

''I trusted her once.''

''Sometimes things don't turn out as we like. Life ain't black and white and folks have to make the best decisions they can. And yes, sometimes, they make the wrong choice and disappoint us. If you give up on Rebecca because she made a mistake she'll regret to her dying day, then you're more a fool than I ever thought.''

Bess yanked out her dust rag from her apron. ''Now I've got to get back to work.'' She walked past him, dismissing him.

Cole smoothed his palms over his thighs. Bess was right in part. Rebecca needed to know Judd was in town and maybe, just maybe, he had been a bit heavy-handed with her earlier.

Resolved, he strode out of the room and toward the stairs. It was time he and Rebecca had that talk.

When Cole strode into Rebecca's room, she sprang up from the edge of the bed. She wiped her moist face with the back of her hand. "Rebecca, we need—"

"How dare you come in here!" She looked up at the ceiling as if someone were there. "He comes in here looking so calm and collected and he's turning my life upside down!"

"Calm down."

She stamped her foot. "Great. Now he's telling me to calm down."

"Rebecca," he said as if talking to a child.

"Get out!" She reached for a book on her night-stand and hurled it at his head.

Cole jerked his body to the right, easily dodging the book that smashed against the wall and fell open-faced on the floor. He advanced a step.

She grabbed another book and threw it. "Go away."

"We've got to talk."

She picked up a small pitcher filled with daises. "You mean you have more orders to issue."

"Dusty's father's back in town."

She lowered the vase and clutched it to her chest. "What!" she whispered. All the fight seemed to drain from her. She squeezed her eyes shut. "Oh, God, not again."

"He's not going to take Dusty." Cole hated seeing her suffer.

Her eyes snapped open. "Did he say that?"

"No. I haven't talked to him yet."

"Then you don't know what he's going to do!"

Panic twisted her features. "I'm going to talk to him. Make him see reason."

Her lips flattened into a grim line and her shoulders slumped. "It was wrong of me to keep the truth from you. Maybe this time—"

"This is a different situation," he said cutting her off. "Judd deserted his boy and in my book that means he surrendered his rights to Dusty."

She slumped forward and buried her face in her hands. "Cole, what are we going to do?" The raw anguish in her voice tore at his heart.

Cole wrapped his arms around her in a protective embrace and pulled her to him. She melted against him and clung to him as if he were a lifeline. She felt good in his arms.

"I swear I won't let him take our boy," he whispered against her ear.

"Our boy." She looked up at him, her eyes misty. "I don't want to lose him."

"He's not going anywhere."

Cole cupped her face in his hands and kissed

her on the lips. The kiss was soft, meant to comfort, but it sent his senses spinning out of control. Dear God, he wanted her.

She whimpered and leaned into the kiss, wrapping her arms around his neck.

He tightened his hold. Her soft curves melded against his body, ignited his desire.

"Make love to me," she whispered.

Needing no more encouragement, he banded his arm around her waist and scooped her legs up with the other. With her cradled in his arms he carried her to the bed and laid her down in the center. Her bed sagged under their weight as he straddled her hips.

She stared up at him, her lips full and moist. She slid trembling hands up his thighs. He sucked in a breath, then captured her hands. He kissed each palm.

Weeks of pent-up emotions begged to be released. He reached for the buttons of her bodice and unfastened each with deliberate slowness. This time he was going to savor touching her, loving her.

Sunlight streamed through the lace curtains onto her creamy white flesh.

Cole cupped her breasts savoring the sight of them. "You're so beautiful," he rasped. He kissed their pink tips until they stood erect.

Rebecca arched toward him, pushing into him. "Cole."

He slid his hand under her skirts and tugged at the drawstring on her pantaloons. The cottony fabric slid easily down her thighs and he reached for her soft feminine flesh. She sucked her breath between clenched teeth when he touched the warm, moist flesh. She was ready for him.

Cole straightened and unfastened the buttons on his pants while Rebecca lay staring up at him, expectant. Her eyes didn't flutter away as he shoved his pants over his narrow hips. Rock hard, he thought he'd explode as she took in the sight of him. Unable to wait, he dropped down on top of her and slid into her.

Rebecca moaned softly, welcoming him inside her. Why was it that when he was inside her he felt so at home, so at peace?

Cole began to move back and forth, letting his primitive side drive him. Rebecca matched him pace for pace, cupping his naked buttocks and sending him teetering to the brink of insanity and pleasure.

Still, he held off. He wanted her to savor the ancient delights. He kissed her nipple and she moaned. He reached for the tender flesh between her legs and began to stroke her. She arched almost immediately. Her husky whispers were inaudible.

"Please Cole, now."

"Not just yet." When they made love they were truly connected and he did not want it to end.

He trailed kisses over her breasts and up the long line of her neck.

He thought he'd burst with wanting her—the exquisite torture. He quickened his pace driving her over the edge into the heart of the maelstrom. Her body stiffened and her fingernails dug into his back. He thrust deep into her and found his own release.

Cole collapsed against her, his body covered in a sheen of sweat. Their heartbeats hammered together as one. And for one instant, he wasn't alone.

He'd survived as long as he had because he had never relied on anyone. He'd come to accept loneliness as inevitable as the sun—but now, he knew he could no longer exist without Rebecca, Mac and Dusty—his family.

Cole rolled off her. They could never be happy until Dusty's custody was resolved and their family safe. He could not begin to mend the rift between them until he'd talked to Judd.

Rebecca trailed her fingers down his back. "Don't go."

"I have to." The simplest touch made him grow hard.

Cole wanted to reach out to her, cradle her in

his arms, but now was not the right time. He had to make certain their family was safe.

"I'm going to look for Judd," he said feeling like he needed to explain.

"What are you going to tell him?"

"The truth."

"Let me come with you."

"This is something I have to do alone."

Rebecca flinched. She gathered the edges of her bodice together. The hurt returned to her eyes. The connection between them was severed, the distance between them returned.

Cole would talk to Judd today—face-to-face, man to man—about Dusty. Judd was a rough sort, and had proved he didn't want the boy. It would be a simple matter to convince the farmer that Dusty belonged with Cole and Rebecca.

It would be simple.

It would be simple.

Rebecca tucked the edges of the comforter under the pillow, still warm from Cole's body. The simple act of making the bed saddened her for smoothing the sheets flat erased all traces of their lovemaking.

And she desperately wanted to cling to the sweet moments when time had stopped and they'd moved as one in a perfect, glorious union.

She touched the pillow where he'd laid his head. It still held the imprint of his head. She picked it up and hugged it to her chest.

If it were possible, Cole's abrupt departure today stung more deeply than it had on their wedding night. He was going to talk to Judd alone, without her. He didn't trust her enough to help.

She laid the pillow back on the bed and walked to the window. What kind of future could they have if he could never trust her?

"Now why are you standing there with such a long face?" Bess's cherry voice echoed from the doorway. "What I wouldn't give to have an afternoon visit like the one you just had. I suppose this means you two have mended the rift between yourselves."

Rebecca shoved her troubled emotions deep inside her and faced her friend. Bess wore a lovely indigo calico and had swept her salt-and-pepper hair into a neat chignon. "Things really haven't changed between us."

"Earning trust takes time."

"I don't know what I can do any differently," she sobbed.

Bess laid her hand on Rebecca's shoulder. "You don't need to do a thing differently. Just keep being there for him. In time he's gonna see what a prize he has for a wife."

"He can't get past my lies."

"He's a prideful man, but in time he'll understand. Have faith in him and your marriage."

Rebecca watched Bess pull a pair of lace gloves from the reticule dangling from her wrist. "Why are you so dressed up? It's not Sunday."

"Ernie's downstairs on the porch waiting for me. He's been promising me a ride in the country for days and I think he's finally gonna see it through."

Rebecca cocked an eyebrow. "Ernie Wade? But I thought the man drove you insane."

"He does, but in a good way. He makes me feel like a young girl."

Rebecca remembered the way Ernie had courted her. "You must have been upset when he came calling on me."

Bess shrugged. "The old coot thought a young wife and a family was what he wanted. If Cole hadn't snapped you up, I would have stepped in and set things straight."

Rebecca smiled. "But you're forever ignoring him."

"Don't pay to let them think you're too interested."

"Ah, Bess," she said hugging her friend. "I wish you two the best."

The older woman grinned and hugged her back. "Thank you."

A loud knock on the front door echoed through the house. Bess giggled like a schoolgirl. "That Ernie is an impatient one."

Rebecca savored her friend's excitement and followed her down the stairs to the front hallway. Ernie stood on the other side of the screened door with a batch of fresh daisies in his meaty fist. His hair was parted down the middle and the distinct smell of bay rum oozed into the house.

"I think he's picked every wildflower in six square miles," Bess whispered.

"Come in, Ernie," Rebecca said chuckling. "You know the way inside."

Ernie opened the door, his gaze flickering briefly from Rebecca to Bess. The wrinkles at his temples deepened when he smiled at Bess. "You're looking might purdy today, Miss Bess."

Bess's skin turned a deep pink. "Thank you."

She tucked her hand in the crook of his arm and he lovingly patted it. "I reckon we'd best be off."

"Where are we going?"

He chucked her under the chin. "Now that's a surprise."

Bess snuggled closed to Ernie. "I love surprises."

He waggled his eyebrows. "I know."

The tender scene tugged at Rebecca's heart. "Make sure you have her back before dark, Ernie Wade."

Bess rolled her eyes. "Rebecca McGuire, I'm old enough to be your mother."

Ernie touched the brim of his hat. "I'll have her back, Mrs. McGuire."

Rebecca grinned. "See that you do."

The couple walked to the picket fence. Ernie opened the gate for Bess. The older woman howled with laughter then sashayed past him. He gave her bottom an affectionate pat and the two walked hand in hand toward town.

Jealousy tugged at Rebecca's heart. That was the way it was supposed to be between a man and woman—a husband and wife—and she wanted that with Cole.

And in that moment, she knew.

She wanted more than Cole's trust. She wanted his love.

Chapter Seventeen

Cole stared at the cracked tumbler full of untouched whiskey. He tapped his fingers against the sticky saloon table as he waited in the darkened corner for Judd. Seth said the farmer had spent most of the morning in the saloon and likely would return soon. Damn, but he hated the waiting.

He reminded himself for the fifth time in the last hour that Judd likely wouldn't give him any trouble. The man had no real use for Dusty. Still, he couldn't quite shake his worries. There was always the chance that Judd wouldn't give him the boy.

He rose from his chair and strode to the swinging doors. He opened it and sucked in the warm afternoon air.

He should have been at the mine. The evening shift would be starting soon. There were walls to be timbered.

But dreams of money and wealth paled now.

His thoughts were only for Dusty, Mac and Rebecca.

His family.

Like Dusty and Mac, he had never belonged anywhere until Rebecca. She had created their family and now was their center, the glue that held them all together.

"You gonna sit there all day nursing that drink?" Seth barked. He sauntered up to the table. His stained apron clung to his wide waist and a bar towel hung over his shoulder.

Cole traced the rim of his glass. "You kicking me out?"

"No." Seth pulled out the seat across from Cole and sat down. "But I've been wondering why a man with such a beautiful wife is sitting in the Rosebud."

"I'm waiting on Judd."

Seth's expression tightened. "I figured as much. If it were me, I'd just wait Judd out. He'll slither back under his rock soon enough. He always does."

"Judd and I need to settle a few things now." He had to be certain his family was safe.

"I don't want any trouble in my saloon."

"There won't be any trouble."

Seth snorted. "You two are trouble waiting to happen."

Cole nodded. He couldn't deny part of him wanted to beat the devil out of Judd—give him a little of what he'd dished out to Dusty. But he'd resolved there would be no trouble, unless it was absolutely necessary.

Seth sighed. "Go on home. I'll send word when he arrives."

"Thanks, but I'll wait here."

Seth straddled a chair across from Cole. "You're worried."

"Nothing I can't handle."

"Boy, you've had more than you could handle since you came back to town."

Cole scowled. "Meaning?"

"Rebecca's done got under your skin."

Silent, Cole sipped his whiskey. The old bastard always had a talent for reading minds.

Seth chuckled. "I remember the way you was when you were with Lily. You was kind and respectful, but your gaze didn't trail her around the room. And you sure never got all tied in knots when she danced with another man."

Cole shifted, uneasy.

"And you could walk away from her without a worry in the world. Now you've gotten tangled up with a woman that you can't walk away from and it scares the hell out of you.''

''Rebecca and I have children. It's a different situation.''

''Men walk away from children all the time.''

''Not me.''

''Rebecca's different. She always has been.''

''You don't know what you're talking about.''

Seth pulled a cheroot from his vest pocket and lit it. ''I remember when you came to town three years ago.'' He inhaled deeply and released a stream of smoke. ''You weren't here to visit your ma's grave or Lily.''

Cole cocked an eyebrow. ''Really? Then why did I come back?''

''To see Rebecca.''

''Bull.''

''I remember how angry you was when you heard she'd eloped. You drank until you couldn't see straight and then you went looking for Lily.''

''What's wrong with a man visiting a friend?''

''She was a substitute.''

''Like hell.''

''Lily was a smart gal. She knew you'd always had eyes for Rebecca.''

''Now, I know you're crazy or drunk.''

''Sane and sober as a judge.''

Cole reached for his hat. "I've heard enough of this."

"I always admired your spunk, even when you was a little fellow. Your ma weren't the best at mothering and I know you suffered for it."

"That's enough, old man." Cole rose but he didn't leave.

"I know you closed off a good part of your soul to get past the hard times, but it's time to open up again."

Cole crushed the brim of his hat in his fist. He'd faced down renegades and outlaws, but never had he been so afraid. It was as if this time, there was more to lose than just his life.

"If you're smart," Seth persisted, "you'll forget about Judd. He'll leave town. Then if you're real smart you'll leave this saloon and go home to your wife. It's where you belong."

The doors to the saloon swung open and Judd staggered in. Covered in dirt, he made his way toward the bar. "Seth! I want a drink."

Seth moved to stand but Cole shook his head. "Let me take this one."

Seth nodded. "Let it go, Cole."

"Sorry, Seth." Cole strode over to Judd who smelled of pigs and urine.

Judd banged his hand against the bar. "Seth!"

Cole tossed his hat on the bar. He reached for a

bottle of whiskey and two glasses. He filled both. "We need to talk."

Judd took one glass and tossed back the whiskey in one gulp. "I ain't got nothing to say to you, McGuire."

"Too bad, you're gonna talk."

Judd rose to his feet. He was a good six inches shorter than Cole, but he was powerfully built, his chest and arms thick with muscles from years of hard labor.

"It's about your boy."

Judd sniffed. "If he's causing trouble don't expect me to fix it."

Cole clenched his fists. "The boy's done nothing wrong."

"Dusty's done nothing *right* since the day he was born."

Cole stared at his knuckles, scraped up this morning while he was wielding a pickax. He flexed his hand as he tried to shake off the urge to ram his fist into Judd's face. "I don't agree."

Judd narrowed his eyes. "I'm not interested in talking about that brat."

"He's living with me and my wife," Cole said tersely.

Judd took Cole's untouched drink and swallowed it. "Wife? Ah, that's right. Some of the boys at the saloon last night said you married that high-

and-mighty Mrs. Taylor. That little miss and I had a run-in this spring. She didn't like the way I was teaching my boy a lesson with the business end of my belt,'' he snarled. ''She's the one that deserved a lesson in keeping her nose out of other people's business.''

If not for the white-hot anger roiling inside him, he'd have enjoyed the flash of pride he felt for his wife. Rebecca was a hellcat when it came to her children.

Still, thinking of her facing Judd alone made his blood run cold. She was no match for him.

Cole kept a tight rein on his emotions, choosing his words carefully so he didn't reveal his anger. Striking a bargain with Judd was more important now than his own anger. ''Rebecca would like Dusty to stay with us.''

Judd bared twin rows of broken yellowed teeth. ''Harvest time will be here before you know it. I'm gonna need his help.''

Again the urge to drive his fist into the farmer's face flared. He held back. ''We aim to raise the boy as our own.''

Judd cackled. ''What the devil would you want to do that for? He's a dirty little beggar who's been nothing but trouble since the day he was born.''

''That's my business.'' Cole tried to swallow the anger that demanded a hunk of Judd's hide. He needed this conversation over and done with before he lost control. "I'll pay you fifty dollars if you promise to leave this town for good and never return."

"Fifty dollars! You're a fool to pay that kind of money for the whelp."

"Is it a deal or not?" Cole said tersely.

Judd scratched his unshaven chin. "Can't say I've ever had that kind of money before."

Cole dug in his vest pocket and pulled out fifty one-dollar bills rolled in a tight wad and tied off with a piece of rawhide. He tossed the money on the bar. "All you have to do is say yes."

Judd licked thin sun-cracked lips. "If you change your mind, I ain't giving the money back." Judd reached for the money, but Cole slammed his hand on top of the farmer's locking it in place.

"Yes."

Cole released the Judd's hand and watched the farmer study the wad of bills before he tucked them in his pocket. "I don't ever want to see you in White Stone again."

Judd smiled. "Reckon I got no reason to come back now."

"Dusty's my child now." Cole had to say the words—he wanted no misunderstandings later.

Judd grabbed a half-full bottle of whiskey from the bar. "Whatever you say."

"Don't ever come back," Cole warned.

Judd laughed and staggered toward the door. "Fool."

Cole watched the farmer push through the doors and down the boardwalk. It wasn't until the man's stocky frame disappeared in the distance that Cole unclenched his fingers and expelled the breath he was holding.

Seth came up behind Cole. "Do you really think you've seen the last of him?"

"Nope."

Judd groaned as he plopped down under a tall oak tree on a small rise looking down on the Shady Grove Inn. The reddish-orange sun hung suspended on the horizon, bathing the town of White Stone and the Shady Grove in an amber light.

He raised the whiskey bottle to his mouth and gulped down the remains of the liquid. He savored the way it burned his throat and dulled the pounding in his head. He wiped the excess whiskey from his lips and stared at the white clapboard house below.

Fifty whole dollars. "Judd, you are one lucky man," he said to himself. Once he'd had five dollars after he'd sold a horse, but never fifty. And it had been the easiest money he'd ever made.

"To think someone as smart as Mr. Cole

McGuire would waste good money on a whelp like Dusty.''

The mountain air had turned cold and Judd hugged the tattered edges of his coat together. He raised the bottle to his lips only to remember it was empty. Angry, he tossed the bottle on the ground. It rolled down the hill toward the inn, crashed into a rock then broke into pieces.

He thought about walking back to the Rosebud and buying another bottle. Then he remembered Cole's warning not to return.

He wasn't up for the long walk to Leadville and even if he did make the fifteen-mile trek, fifty dollars wouldn't buy so much whiskey in a boomtown. ''Hell, I'd be lucky if I could get three bottles of good booze for fifty bucks.''

Irritated, he thought back to the deal he'd struck with Cole. The delight he'd felt soured. Maybe he'd been too quick to accept McGuire's offer.

He glared at the lantern light that glowed from the inn's windows. People who lived in houses like that had more money than they could shake a stick at. Probably, fifty dollars was nothing to the likes of them.

''Damn it all,'' Judd muttered. ''If you'd been smart you'd have held out for seventy-five, maybe one hundred dollars.''

Just then Rebecca McGuire's slim figure moved

in front of a lighted window. He leaned forward, unable to take his eyes off her.

Dressed in a thick blue robe, she stared up at the starlit sky, her long blond hair draping over her shoulders. She was a beauty. Stuck-up as they came, but Judd couldn't deny that she made a man yearn for more.

Dusty ran up to Rebecca. She brushed the hair off the boy's smiling face then hugged him close. Something inside Judd tightened with fury.

It wasn't right that the brat had a fine house to sleep in while all he had was fifty stinking dollars. His hostility grew when he considered all the years he'd clothed and fed that boy.

"Dusty don't deserve to live high on the hog when his old man don't have squat."

He reached in his pocket and pulled out the roll of dollars. He deserved better. "Years of back-breaking labor has only gotten me pennies for my trouble while the McGuires of the world get rich and have little wives to warm their beds."

Rebecca McGuire pulled the curtains closed.

Judd flinched and swallowed a lump in his throat. "Here you is again, shut out of the good life."

McGuire hadn't been the fool. He had been, for selling out so quick.

The farmer pulled himself to his feet. "Seeing

as Mr. McGuire ain't home, it seems only proper I pay his wife a call.''

Rebecca laughed as she kissed Mac for the tenth time in five minutes. The light of her lantern glowed from a bedside table onto the twin beds where the boys lay, tucked in and ready for bed. ''No, it's time you go to bed.''

''Mama, stay.''

Dusty stuck out his lip. ''Oh, please read us one more story.''

''You two sidewinders have already wheedled enough of a reprieve. It's bedtime.''

''Mama,'' Mac yelled.

''Come on, Ma, just one more story.''

Rebecca's heart hitched a notch. Dusty had never called her Ma before. She walked over to his bed and kissed him on the forehead. ''I love you.'' She winked at him. ''But good night.''

The boys moaned and groaned as she walked out of the room, lantern in hand, and closed the door. She hesitated, listening until their giggles grew quiet.

The house was silent expect for the chimes of the grandfather clock that marked seven o'clock. Save for the buttery glow of her lantern, it was dark.

Normally she welcomed the quiet in the evenings, but since her marriage her loneliness was most keen at this time. This was the time reserved for husbands and wives.

She tightened her shawl around her and went downstairs. A cup of tea would ease her worries.

As she came down the hallway, she noticed the flicker of candlelight from the kitchen. She frowned. Cole rarely made it home before midnight and Bess wasn't due back from her evening with the sheriff for at least an hour.

Holding her lantern high, she called out, "Cole."

She froze on the threshold to the kitchen. Judd Saunders sat at her kitchen table, a six-shooter and an uncorked bottle of sherry in front of him.

He grinned, baring yellowed broken teeth. "Evening, Mrs. McGuire."

Rebecca bit back a wave of panic. Her first thought was for the children tucked in their beds upstairs. Her second was for the gun hidden in the pantry. She had to get it.

Judd raised the bottle to his lips and took a swig. "Join me for a drink, Mrs. McGuire."

"No, thank you, Judd," she said, careful to keep all traces of fear from her voice.

He snarled and glared at her with the eyes of a rattler. "I ain't asking, I'm telling."

Rebecca's breathing slowed. She heard the

pounding of her heart in her ears as she took a seat across the table from him. Her nose wrinkled as she got a whiff of pigs. "What can I do for you this evening?"

He pushed the bottle toward her. "Have a drink."

"I don't drink."

"Drink!" he shouted.

She started and reached for the bottle with trembling hands. She wiped the mouth of the bottle with her hand and took a sip and quickly set it back down. "Why are you here, Judd?"

"I come to collect my boy."

Her throat tightened. "He's not here."

Judd grinned. "Now, don't you start lying to ol' Judd. I don't much take to that."

Fear chilled her heart. "I'm not lying."

"I saw him through this here window," he said pointing over his shoulder, "not a half hour ago."

She wished she'd paid closer attention to Cole's instructions regarding the shotgun now. "He left."

Judd slammed the sherry bottle against the table. Amber liquid sloshed on his dirty hands. He rose. His powerfully built shoulders loomed as he advanced toward her.

The muscles in her back bunched into tight knots. "Judd, don't take him. He's happy and doing so well."

"You think I care if that brat is happy?" He jabbed his meaty thumb into his chest. "Ain't nobody worried if Judd's happy or not."

She stood and took a step back. The shotgun was less than fifteen feet from her, tucked up on the top shelf, but it might as well have been a mile away. She'd never retrieve the gun before Judd acted.

Judd staggered forward. "What's going on in that purdy little head of yours Mrs. High-and-Mighty?"

She forced her nerves to calm. She glanced at the half-full bottle of sherry on the table. "You're right, Judd."

"What do you mean?" he snarled.

"No one is looking after you." If she could connect with him, perhaps she could persuade him to leave. "Perhaps, I could get you something better to drink. Brandy, perhaps." She turned toward the pantry.

"Hold it right there, little missy. You think I'm stupid? You thinking you can just slip away from ol' Judd?" He grabbed her by the arm. "Or maybe you're thinking if I get good and liquored up, I'll pass out."

"No." She tried to twist free from his iron grip.

"Well, I ain't stupid. Fact, I'm getting smarter with each hour. You and your husband think you're so smart, but you ain't. McGuire's a fool to think he could buy my boy from me for fifty dollars.'' Shadows slashed across his craggy face giving him a more menacing look.

"Cole paid you money."

Judd pulled the wad of bills from his pocket and shoved them in her face. "That's what your man thinks Dusty's worth. Only I figured out that that kid's worth a whole lot more."

"That child is priceless."

Judd laughed. "I was gonna say he's worth about one hundred dollars."

"I don't have that kind of money."

He wrenched her arm tighter, jerking her against his fleshy body. "Everybody in this town knows you got more money than you know what to do with."

"You're wrong! My first husband took it all."

"Then you better come up with something ol' Judd wants or I'm taking my boy back."

"No!" she shouted. Her mind raced as she inventoried the belongings in her house. "I don't have any money, but I've a few pieces of jewelry hidden in the sugar jar in the pantry."

"What good is jewels? I can't eat or drink those."

"You could sell them."

He seemed to consider her proposal. His oily

gaze slid over her. A smile tugged at the corner of his lips. "You got anything else?"

She clutched the ends of her shawl together. "No."

He pushed her forward. "Get 'em."

She stumbled the few steps into pantry. Trembling, she stood on tiptoe and skimmed her hands over the top shelf.

Judd shoved her shoulder. "Hurry up, I ain't got all day." He loomed over her, watching, waiting. Then her fingers slid over cold metal. The gun!

Praying for courage, she wrapped her fingers around the cold barrel and in one fluid movement jerked the gun down, swung around and pointed it at Judd. "Get back," she said.

Judd backed out of the pantry. "You expect me to believe you can shoot a gun? You ain't got the backbone to draw blood."

"Don't count on it."

Judd laughed and shook his head. "And here I thought we was seeing eye to eye. I thought you was gonna be nice to ol' Judd."

"Get out of my house. If you ever come back here again, I'll kill you." She followed him into the kitchen.

He held up his hands in surrender. "Well, I sure don't want to get a gut full of buckshot. I'm leaving. No need to shoot." He turned.

Her shoulder relaxed only a fraction, but Judd took advantage. As fast as a rattler, he whirled around and snatched the gun from her hands. His eyes glowed with unchecked rage. He pointed the weapon at her. For several seconds they stared at each other—she too frightened to move, he struggling with some inner demon.

"Judd, please, we are not worth your trouble."

"The hell you ain't." He raised the gun higher. Twin barrels were only inches from her head.

Rebecca held up her hands in defense seconds before he turned the gun around and cracked the butt against her head.

Blinding pain knocked her to the floor. Bile rose in her throat as she fought to stay conscious. When she raised her head, she feared it would split in two. Blood trickled down her forehead and she collapsed against the cold pine floor.

Her last thoughts were for her children and Cole before her world went black.

Chapter Eighteen

Rage. Fury. Madness.

There was no word to describe the feelings inside Cole as he looked through the kitchen window and saw Rebecca lying unconscious on the kitchen floor and Judd standing over her. Bright lantern light shone on her bruised forehead and a fine trickle of blood trailing down her cheek. His heart constricted as if a fist squeezed the very life out of it.

A savage urge to wrap his fingers around Judd's neck and choke the life out of him surged through Cole's body. But he held back. Judd had a gun pointed at his wife and he didn't know where the children were.

Cole thanked God he'd been too filled with thoughts of Rebecca to work and had left the mine shortly after the second shift had started.

Rebecca moaned then and stirred. Slowly, she pushed herself into a sitting position. She touched her finger to her temple and winced.

Cole would have dropped to his knees and said words of thanks, if he'd had the luxury. Instead, he slid his gun from its holster.

Judd sneered. "Maybe that'll teach you to mess with ol' Judd." A note of glee in his voice confirmed he liked preying on the weak and hurting those who couldn't strike back.

Rebecca's gaze was sure and direct when she met his. "What do you want?"

Judd scratched the thick stubble on his skin. "Seeing as I ain't in no rush to leave now, maybe we could get to know each other better."

If his wife was afraid, Cole couldn't see any signs of fear. She didn't flinch or cower. Damn, but he was proud of her.

She brushed a lock of hair off her face. "My husband will be home soon."

"I hear tell he works late every evening."

"He's gonna kill you when he finds out you were here."

"If he can catch me."

Cole wrapped his long fingers around the white knob on the back door and turned it to the right. He eased the door open and took three silent steps toward Judd.

The wind rustled outside. Judd must have realized something wasn't right because he whirled around, shotgun in hand. He growled when he saw Cole. "Come near me and I'll kill her." To emphasize his point he jabbed the tip of the gun at Rebecca.

Cole froze. He needed ice water in his veins if he was going to save Rebecca and the children.

Wildness clouded Judd's eyes. "I'll do it."

Cole's lips curled into a menacing grin. "And then you'll die."

Rebecca cradled her head. "I told you he was going to come. You will be sorry if you don't put that gun down and walk out of here."

Judd shook his head. "He's never gonna let me walk outta here." Sweat beaded on his forehead. "He's the one that's going to be sorry. I deserve better than what I got."

Cole advanced a step, a taste for blood in his mouth now. "So did Dusty."

Judd's gaze shot back up to Cole. "Get back."

"Make me."

Like any bully, Judd wasn't accustomed to being challenged. Fear flickered for just an instant in his black eyes. He was afraid and they both knew it.

Judd snarled and pulled back the hammer of the gun as Cole fired twice. He hit Judd in the shoulder and sent him slamming against the wall, the tip of his gun jerking up. As Judd fell, his finger squeezed the trigger and he sprayed the ceiling with buckshot before he dropped to the floor, bleeding, unconscious, but alive.

Cole's shoulder burned. He'd been hit, but didn't stop to worry over it. Blood oozed over his hands as he snatched the shotgun away from Judd's limp hands. He rolled the man on his back, making certain he was no longer a threat.

Satisfied, he hurried to Rebecca, dropped to his knees and cradled her in his arms. "Rebecca, are you all right?"

She clung to him. "Yes."

"Did he hurt you?"

"No," she choked out.

If he lived to be one hundred, he'd never be more thankful than he was at this moment. He hugged her fiercely against his chest. "When I saw him standing over you, I thought I'd go insane."

Rebecca's head pounded so. She stared up at Cole. She'd never been gladder to see his grim, tight-lipped face. He was her savior, her protector, and for the first time in such a long time, she wasn't alone.

She raised her chin. She wanted to cry tears born of joy and relief, but she refused. "He wanted to take Dusty."

Cole glanced down at Judd, still unconscious. "I never would have let that happen."

"They were sleeping upstairs. I tried to get the gun, but he took it away from me."

"Shh. It doesn't matter now. The only thing I care about is that you and the boys are safe."

"The boys. I better go check on them." She tried to stand, but her head pounded. Her stomach lurched. Her mouth tasted bitter and for a moment she thought she'd retch.

Cole held her tight. "Easy there. We'll check on the boys together as soon as I tie Judd up."

She nodded and rose. Her head spun and it took an instant for her to steady herself as Cole found a length of rope in the kitchen and tied Judd's hands and feet.

When Cole faced her she noticed the blood on his shirt. "You've been shot."

"I'm fine."

She touched his bloodstained shoulder. "You're not fine. You're bleeding."

"The boys first."

"And then I bandage you."

He chuckled. "You're in no shape to nurse anyone."

She wobbled as they climbed the stairs. "I'm okay."

"We'll just see about that."

Arm in arm they made their way up to the nursery. Cole eased the door open and found Dusty and Mac asleep, right where Rebecca had left them earlier.

"Thank God," she murmured, amazed the noise had not woken them.

Cole strode over to Dusty and touched his back, counting the rise and fall of his back as he breathed. He stared at Dusty a long moment as he lay sleeping on his stomach, one foot sticking out from the blanket and his face buried in the pillow. He bent down and kissed the child then turned to Mac.

"Thank you, God, for letting me be the father to these boys," he whispered as he tucked Mac's blanket up to his chin and kissed him on the forehead.

Rebecca's heart constricted. She'd never loved her husband more than she did right now.

Cole's expression was somber when he joined her. He wrapped his arm around her shoulder and the two lingered in the doorway another moment.

She drew comfort from his firm grip. "I couldn't live without them."

"Me, either." Cole ran his fingers over a bump on her forehead. "And I couldn't live without you, Rebecca."

Worry lines framed his mouth and eyes. His

cheeks were sunken and drawn and his hair a wild mess. He looked ten years older. "Oh, Cole."

"I love you, Rebecca. I think I always have."

Tears stung her eyes.

"I came home tonight to tell you I'm sorry. I understand why you lied about Mac. You were doing what was best for him. I can see that now. Your love for him is part of the reason I love you so much."

She touched his face, rough and unshaved. "I was afraid you'd never trust me again."

He cupped her chin in his rough hand and stared into her eyes. "I trust you with my life."

"I love you, Cole." Tears streamed down her face, her promise not to cry forgotten.

He hugged her against his chest. "I've waited a lifetime to hear those words from you and I swear I'll never get tired of hearing them."

She smiled. "Good, because I plan to say it often."

A chuckle rumbled in his chest. "At least once a day."

"Maybe twice."

He traced her lips with his finger. His expression grew pensive. "You are the center of my life, Rebecca. You are the heart of this family. Without you I am nothing."

"*We* are the heart of this family, Cole. And *we* are nothing without each other."

A shadow of a smile touched his mouth. His expression was filled with tenderness and promised a future filled with happiness, laughter and love. They would love each other with a searing passion and raise their boys together to be strong and proud men.

Epilogue

Eight Years Later

Ernie Wade had carted Judd off to jail that night. He was charged with attempted murder and assault. Ernie kept him in the jail twelve days before the judge made it back to town for the trial. It took the twelve-man jury ten minutes to convict Judd and sentence him to twenty years in prison. The judge decreed Dusty would stay with Cole and Rebecca.

Cole recovered quickly from his wounds and within three days he was back at the mine supervising his crews.

Twenty-seven days after Cole had reopened the Lucky Star, they found silver. Now, most folks will tell you it wasn't the richest vein in Colorado history, but most reckon it was in the top ten.

Ernie and Bess married on Christmas Day of

that same year. And nine months to the day they welcomed baby John into the world.

Hard to believe so much time had passed as Rebecca watched her husband and four sons standing on the dais next to the governor in town today for the ribbon cutting of White Stone's new courthouse.

Dusty stood next to Cole and his brothers Mac, Leo and Lee. Dusty, eighteen years old now, had been accepted to the University of Virginia. Rebecca's heart tightened with love when she thought about her oldest son going so far from home, but Dusty craved the challenge of a university education. His dark hair and magnetic eyes had caught the attention of more than one young girl and he promised to be a real heartbreaker.

Eleven-year-old Mac continued to excel at White Stone's new schoolhouse, which boasted four rooms now, though he was quick to tell anyone who would listen that he preferred fishing. Next to him stood his younger brothers, six-year-old Leo and seven-year-old Lee. The boys had arrived in White Stone five years ago on the orphan train. Both boys had hair the color of sand and eyes as green as grass. They had a zest for riding and wide-open spaces and both had an incurable taste for peppermints.

The McGuire men were individuals, each with strong personalities. The one trait they all shared was a fierce protectiveness of Rebecca and their baby sister, six-month-old Lily.

Rebecca stared into her daughter's face. She had Cole's black hair and her blue eyes and the infant was indeed a miracle. She smoothed her gloved finger over the little girl's nose and puckered lips.

Just then the crowd cheered. Cole waved to the crowd and climbed down from the dais. He stopped to shake a few hands then cut through the crowd toward Rebecca.

His eyes sparkled and his lips quirked into a seductive smile. With his shoulders back, he swaggered toward her. Delicious warmth spread through her body and her mind skipped forward to tonight when he would take her in his arms and make love to her.

He came to her side and wrapped his arm possessively around her shoulder. He kissed Lily on her forehead then in a voice only Rebecca could hear said, "Is it my imagination, Mrs. McGuire, or did you just have an impure thought about the town's new mayor?"

Her laugh was throaty, seductive. "I'm afraid so, *Mayor* McGuire."

He nibbled her earlobe, sending a thousand tiny tremors skidding down her spine. "Good. Hold that thought."

* * * * *

Enchanted by England?

Take a journey through the British Isles with Harlequin Historicals

ON SALE JULY 2001

THE PROPER WIFE
by **Julia Justiss**
Sequel to **THE WEDDING GAMBLE**
(England, 1814)

MAGIC AND MIST
by **Theresa Michaels**
Book three in the Clan Gunn series
(Scotland & Wales, 1384)

MY LORD SAVAGE
by **Elizabeth Lane**
(England, 1580s)

ON SALE AUGUST 2001

CELTIC BRIDE
by **Margo Maguire**
(England, 1428)

LADY POLLY
by **Nicola Cornick**
Sequel to **THE VIRTUOUS CYPRIAN**
(England, 1817)

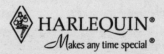

HARLEQUIN®
*M*akes any time special ®

*Harlequin truly does
make any time special....
This year we are celebrating
weddings in style!*

A Walk Down the Aisle

WEDDING CELEBRATION

To help us celebrate, we want you to tell us how wearing the Harlequin wedding gown will make your wedding day special. As the grand prize, Harlequin will offer one lucky bride the chance to **"Walk Down the Aisle"** in the Harlequin wedding gown!

There's more...

For her honeymoon, she and her groom will spend five nights at the **Hyatt Regency Maui.** As part of this five-night honeymoon at the hotel renowned for its romantic attractions, the couple will enjoy a candlelit dinner for two in Swan Court, a sunset sail on the hotel's catamaran, and duet spa treatments.

A HYATT RESORT AND SPA

Maui • Molokai • Lanai

To enter, please write, in, 250 words or less, how wearing the Harlequin wedding gown will make your wedding day special. The entry will be judged based on its emotionally compelling nature, its originality and creativity, and its sincerity. This contest is open to Canadian and U.S. residents only and to those who are 18 years of age and older. There is no purchase necessary to enter. Void where prohibited. See further contest rules attached. Please send your entry to:

Walk Down the Aisle Contest

In Canada	In U.S.A.
P.O. Box 637	P.O. Box 9076
Fort Erie, Ontario	3010 Walden Ave.
L2A 5X3	Buffalo, NY 14269-9076

You can also enter by visiting www.eHarlequin.com
Win the Harlequin wedding gown and the vacation of a lifetime!
The deadline for entries is October 1, 2001.

HARLEQUIN®
Makes any time special ®

PHWDACONT1

1. To enter, follow directions published in the offer to which you are responding. Contest begins April 2, 2001, and ends on October 1, 2001. Method of entry may vary. Mailed entries must be postmarked by October 1, 2001, and received by October 8, 2001.

2. Contest entry may be, at times, presented via the Internet, but will be restricted solely to residents of certain geographic areas that are disclosed on the Web site. To enter via the Internet, if permissible, access the Harlequin Web site (www.eHarlequin.com) and follow the directions displayed online. Online entries must be received by 11:59 p.m. E.S.T. on October 1, 2001.

   In lieu of submitting an entry online, enter by mail by hand-printing (or typing) on an 8½" x 11" plain piece of paper, your name, address (including zip code), Contest number/name and in 250 words or fewer, why winning a Harlequin wedding dress would make your wedding day special. Mail via first-class mail to: Harlequin Walk Down the Aisle Contest 1197, (in the U.S.) P.O. Box 9076, 3010 Walden Avenue, Buffalo, NY 14269-9076, (in Canada) P.O. Box 637, Fort Erie, Ontario L2A 5X3, Canada.

   Limit one entry per person, household address and e-mail address. Online and/or mailed entries received from persons residing in geographic areas in which Internet entry is not permissible will be disqualified.

3. Contests will be judged by a panel of members of the Harlequin editorial, marketing and public relations staff based on the following criteria:
   - Originality and Creativity—50%
   - Emotionally Compelling—25%
   - Sincerity—25%

   In the event of a tie, duplicate prizes will be awarded. Decisions of the judges are final.

4. All entries become the property of Torstar Corp. and will not be returned. No responsibility is assumed for lost, late, illegible, incomplete, inaccurate, nondelivered or misdirected mail or misdirected e-mail, for technical, hardware or software failures of any kind, lost or unavailable network connections, or failed, incomplete, garbled or delayed computer transmission or any human error which may occur in the receipt or processing of the entries in this Contest.

5. Contest open only to residents of the U.S. (except Puerto Rico) and Canada, who are 18 years of age or older, and is void wherever prohibited by law; all applicable laws and regulations apply. Any litigation within the Province of Quebec respecting the conduct or organization of a publicity contest may be submitted to the Régie des alcools, des courses et des jeux for a ruling. Any litigation respecting the awarding of a prize may be submitted to the Régie des alcools, des courses et des jeux only for the purpose of helping the parties reach a settlement. Employees and immediate family members of Torstar Corp. and D. L. Blair, Inc., their affiliates, subsidiaries and all other agencies, entities and persons connected with the use, marketing or conduct of this Contest are not eligible to enter. Taxes on prizes are the sole responsibility of winners. Acceptance of any prize offered constitutes permission to use winner's name, photograph or other likeness for the purposes of advertising, trade and promotion on behalf of Torstar Corp., its affiliates and subsidiaries without further compensation to the winner, unless prohibited by law.

6. Winners will be determined no later than November 15, 2001, and will be notified by mail. Winners will be required to sign and return an Affidavit of Eligibility form within 15 days after winner notification. Noncompliance within that time period may result in disqualification and an alternative winner may be selected. Winners of trip must execute a Release of Liability prior to ticketing and must possess required travel documents (e.g. passport, photo ID) where applicable. Trip must be completed by November 2002. No substitution of prize permitted by winner. Torstar Corp. and D. L. Blair, Inc., their parents, affiliates, and subsidiaries are not responsible for errors in printing or electronic presentation of Contest, entries and/or game pieces. In the event of printing or other errors which may result in unintended prize values or duplication of prizes, all affected game pieces or entries shall be null and void. If for any reason the Internet portion of the Contest is not capable of running as planned, including infection by computer virus, bugs, tampering, unauthorized intervention, fraud, technical failures, or any other causes beyond the control of Torstar Corp. which corrupt or affect the administration, secrecy, fairness, integrity or proper conduct of the Contest, Torstar Corp. reserves the right, at its sole discretion, to disqualify any individual who tampers with the entry process and to cancel, terminate, modify or suspend the Contest or the Internet portion thereof. In the event of a dispute regarding an online entry, the entry will be deemed submitted by the authorized holder of the e-mail account submitted at the time of entry. Authorized account holder is defined as the natural person who is assigned to an e-mail address by an Internet access provider, online service provider or other organization that is responsible for arranging e-mail address for the domain associated with the submitted e-mail address. **Purchase or acceptance of a product offer does not improve your chances of winning.**

7. Prizes: (1) Grand Prize—A Harlequin wedding dress (approximate retail value: $3,500) and a 5-night/6-day honeymoon trip to Maui, HI, including round-trip air transportation provided by Maui Visitors Bureau from Los Angeles International Airport (winner is responsible for transportation to and from Los Angeles International Airport) and a Harlequin Romance Package, including hotel accomodations (double occupancy) at the Hyatt Regency Maui Resort and Spa, dinner for (2) two at Swan Court, a sunset sail on Kiele V and a spa treatment for the winner (approximate retail value: $4,000); (5) Five runner-up prizes of a $1000 gift certificate to selected retail outlets to be determined by Sponsor (retail value $1000 ea.). Prizes consist of only those items listed as part of the prize. Limit one prize per person. All prizes are valued in U.S. currency.

8. For a list of winners (available after December 17, 2001) send a self-addressed, stamped envelope to: Harlequin Walk Down the Aisle Contest 1197 Winners, P.O. Box 4200 Blair, NE 68009-4200 or you may access the www.eHarlequin.com Web site through January 15, 2002.

Contest sponsored by Torstar Corp., P.O. Box 9042, Buffalo, NY 14269-9042, U.S.A.

PHWDACONT2

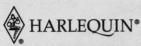 

USA Today bestselling author

STELLA CAMERON

and popular American Romance author

MURIEL JENSEN

come together in a special
Harlequin 2-in-1 collection.

Look for

Shadows and *Daddy in Demand*

On sale June 2001

HARLEQUIN®

Makes any time special ®